VICTORY

VICTORY

SUSAN COOPER

SCHOLASTIC INC.
New York Toronto London Auckland Sydney
Mexico City New Delhi Hong Kong Buenos Aires

ISBN-13: 978-0-545-07438-4
ISBN-10: 0-545-07438-X

12 11 10 9 8 7 6 5 4   12 13/0

Printed in the U.S.A.   40

First Scholastic printing, March 2008

Book design by Ann Zeak

The text for this book is set in Fournier.

Lexile is a registered trademark of MetaMetrics, Inc.

For Dudley

in affectionate memory
and in return for
"Ramage's Diamond"

LORD NELSON
Engraving from a portrait by John Hoppner, 1801, used as
a frontispiece in *The Life of Nelson* by Robert Southey.
National Portrait Gallery, London

Full fathom five thy father lies;
Of his bones are coral made;
Those are pearls that were his eyes;
Nothing of him that doth fade
But doth suffer a sea-change
Into something rich and strange. . . .

The Tempest
William Shakespeare

*T*he sound of the drums was like the beating of a great slow heart. Muffled drums, they were, with black cloth over them. Everything was muffled that day, even the grey clouded sky. All of England was mourning the death of one man, and all the people of London were out on the streets leading to St. Paul's, and all the air filled with the slow beat of those drums and the unending slow march of thousands of feet.

Ten thousand soldiers marched in procession that day, before and behind us, in that long step that they keep for funerals, with the hesitation in it that breaks your heart. Marines were marching too, and the cavalry regiments trotting their horses slow, with a soft jingle of harness, and artillery with horses pulling the creaking gun carriages. Every man of us wore black stockings, with black crepe on our hats, and black ribbons hung from the horses' heads. Over the beat of the drums, sometimes you would hear the wailing lament of a pipe band, like London weeping.

And there were we, forty-eight of us from the crew of his flagship HMS Victory, walking in pairs: forty-eight seamen and marines, with the senior men up front carrying our poor flag, the tattered white ensign that had flown from the masthead at the Battle of Trafalgar and been shot through and through. The men held it up sometimes to show it to the people lining the streets, and some said you could hear a rustle like the sound of the sea as *hundreds and hundreds of men took off their hats in respect. Me, all I could hear was the drums, and the feet, and the boom of the minute guns.*

Dozens of carriages creaked along behind us, drawn by more jingling horses, filled with noblemen and officers. Thirty-two admirals in full dress uniform there were at the Admiral's funeral, and a hundred captains. There never was a funeral like it, not even for a king. The Prince of Wales rode in his crested carriage just in front of the funeral car, a long gun carriage made to look like our Victory, with high prow and stern, and a canopy swaying above our Admiral's coffin.

With music and high words the funeral service lasted for hours, inside St. Paul's Cathedral. A great blaze of candles hung from the huge domed roof. At the very end, when the coffin was to be lowered into the ground, we seamen had been told to fold our ensign in ceremony, and lay it on the top. But when Will Wilmet the bosun and three of the older men took up that shredded white cloth, Will gave a kind of sob—and suddenly all the men were reaching for our sad flag and it came apart, and they stuffed pieces of it into their jackets. And the coffin went down into the crypt, under the stone floor, forever.

He was a good man, Wilmet. He gave me a scrap of the flag for my own, afterward, outside the Cathedral, when we were gathering to march back through the streets of London without our Admiral.

"Here, young Sam," he said. "Here's a bit for you. Keep it till you die, and have it buried with you. Your own little bit of Nelson."

Molly

❧

AUGUST 2006

MOLLY SITS IN A CONNECTICUT GARDEN WITH HER BOOK, UNDER A TOWERING MAPLE TREE. *"CHEEOO, CHEEOO, CHEEOO,"* sings a cardinal from the branches above her, a high clear call, and somewhere far off another bird answers him. Then the bird flies, swooping down and across the lawn past the garden chair on which Molly sits: a bright red flash of a bird, like none she ever saw at home.

But this is home now, she tries to remind herself.

Never, says a rebellious small voice silently in her brain.

Something drops past her nose in a blur, and she looks down and sees a hairy caterpillar moving smartly across the page, rippling, hasty. Now she knows what that litter of tiny black dots on the arm of her chair must be: droppings from hairy caterpillars.

"Yuck!" says Molly and shakes the caterpillar down onto the grass. Maybe the singing bird will come back and have it for tea.

There's no such meal as tea, here, says the small silent voice.

Molly is an English city girl. All her eleven years until this one have been spent in London—though London is greener than most cities, full of parks and trees, and squares with gardens in the middle. Molly and her mother had lived in one such, in Merton Square. The Victorian terraced houses on all four sides of the square had long been divided into apartments, and theirs was on the top floor. In the center of the square was a garden the size of a football field, set about with trees and flowerbeds and small lawns. The whole garden was enclosed behind wrought-iron fencing, with two big iron gates to which every family who lived in the square—but nobody else—had a key. Though Molly was a city girl, her bedroom looked out over treetops.

But that was then. This is now, in Connecticut, four thousand miles away. Molly brushes a few new black dots off the page of her book, and sighs. The book is part of her summer reading for the school she will go to in September. It is a novel about Paul Revere, hero of the Revolutionary War, the war in which the noble American patriots wrested their freedom from the tyrannical British. Molly finds Paul Revere boringly virtuous. She misses King Alfred who burned the cakes, King Canute who vainly told the sea to go back, King Charles who lost his head; she misses two thousand years of imperfect British heroes.

"Molly!" It is her mother's voice calling from the house, over the new-cut, sweet-smelling lawn. She sounds harassed. "Moll! Come and give me a hand, love!"

Molly runs indoors. The air-conditioned house is cold, after the soft heat of the sunlit garden. In the big white kitchen her baby brother Donald is clamped into his high chair, picking up bits of avocado with amazing delicacy between finger and thumb. He catches sight of her, and beams. "Mowy!" he cries, and whacks a chubby hand down on his plastic table, smashing the avocado into a gooey mess.

"Feed him, darling, would you?" Kate Hibbert says, handing her daughter the bowl of baby-sized bits of chicken and vegetables. "I'm making sandwiches—Carl and Russell are coming home for lunch. They've put the boat in the water, they're all cock-a-hoop, they want to take you for a sail."

Molly's heart sinks, but she makes a happy face at Donald and slips a morsel of chicken into his birdlike open mouth. "I have to finish Paul Revere," she says.

Kate glances at her, as she opens the refrigerator for bread, mayonnaise, ham, sliced cheese. She understands, and at the same time she's making a demand. "Be nice, darling," she says.

The wind is blowing briskly off Long Island Sound, and the sailboat heels sharply to the right. Carl hauls at the mainsheet to hold her closer into the wind, and the boat creams through the water, the waves going *slap-slap-slap* against her sides. Tilted sideways and jolted up and down, Molly presses her bottom against the edge of the boat's side where Carl has put her, on the left.

Port, she says to herself silently. *Port is left. Starboard is right. The edge is the gunwale. When he says "Ready about," get over the other side. To starboard. Right.*

Next to her, her stepbrother Russell grips the jib-sheet, his tanned face tipped up to the sky and the wind. He's loving it all; he's been doing this since he was a baby. He glances at her sideways. "You okay?" he says.

Carl says, "Ready about!"

"Duck your head!" says Russell, and in an uneasy scramble Molly gets herself under the boom, as the mainsail swings across the boat with a flapping rattle of canvas and line. She bangs her elbow against the mast, she gets in Russell's way as he pulls the jib to the other side. Scuffling her feet, clutching at the gunwale, she tries dutifully, desperately to lean backward as the deck tilts away from her. The boat is alive, strong, swift as a galloping horse in this noisy companionship with the wind. Molly has a hollow feeling at the pit of her stomach; it is not seasickness, it is fear. She longs to be back on dry land.

Carl yells to her, "Want to take the tiller?"

"Noooo!" Molly says in appalled honesty, and he laughs. He looks totally happy, like his son. Carl is a lean, tall man with a face creased by smiling, and thinning hair flattened against his head now by the wind. He has been her stepfather for two years, yet she feels she does not know him very well.

Molly scarcely remembers her real father; he died in a plane crash when she was four years old. All her life after that, she and Kate were a two-person team, coping with the balance between Kate's job and Molly's school, times with Granny and Grandad and times with friends, all in the embrace of London's brick and stone and trees. This lasted until the day when Kate took up with smiling American Carl Hibbert, the widower with the son five years older than Molly—Russell, who still treats her like a baby even now, two years after their parents stunned them both by getting married.

In the beginning, they all four lived in London, where Carl ran the European office of the big American company for which he works. Kate became pregnant and had Donald, whom Molly adores and Russell tries to ignore. Molly still went to her Kensington school, Russell to the American School in London, and they all led a fairly amiable two-pronged life, these two Brits and two Yanks. Until another day, when Carl's company moved him back to the United States, and his family had to go too, and Molly's life fell apart.

"Ready about!" Carl calls unexpectedly, and Molly is suddenly at a loss, forgetting what she should do. Russell is busy with the jib, shifting himself and the sail to the other side of the boat. Carl is juggling tiller and mainsheet. So nobody yells a warning to Molly to duck, as the tall sail on the heavy boom swings across and a wave tips the boat, and the boom catches her off balance and knocks her over the side, into the sea.

Panic fills her like a scream as the cold water closes over her head. She comes up gasping, flailing; a wave smacks her face, she can see nothing but green water. Her sneakers are like lead weights on her feet, dragging her legs down when she tries to kick. She gasps and gasps and makes terrible sounds as the sea forces water into her lungs. She is sure she is about to drown.

Someone is behind her, hands under her arms, yelling words she cannot hear. Russell is in the water with her. Frantic, Molly tries to clutch at him; he forces her to turn away from him. A wave breaks over them both. Molly is gurgling, choking, but the hands holding her from behind are keeping her head up out of the water. She glimpses the side of the boat nearby, tossing, enormous; hears the loud flapping of the sail, sees Carl moving fast, reaching a hand down toward her.

Somehow, pulling, pushing, they get her over the side of the tossing boat and she lies there coughing up water, drawing in whistling breaths. She is a mess of terror and relief and misery, dripping, cold. Russell drags himself into the boat and drops almost on top of her. He pushes wet dark hair out of his eyes. He grins at her.

"Thank—you—" Molly croaks, and throws up seawater, and weeps.

Russell's still grinning. "You've had your turn!" he yells over the noise of the sails.

"Get the jib!" Carl snaps. He is pushing at the tiller, fighting with the other hand to haul in the mainsail, to get this prancing disorderly racehorse back to its frightening smooth speed.

Russell grabs the flapping line and hauls the jib into stillness, in line with the big sail as it steadies and fills. Even now he is clearly enjoying himself. He yells to Molly, "Everyone goes over once! You'll never do it again!"

Molly says fervently, "You bet I won't!" She is lying there making resolutions never, ever, to find herself on this boat again.

So they sail on, carried fast through the choppy water by the pressure of the wind fighting the sail. Russell and his father are both feeling vaguely guilty that they did not take time for the extra moment of caution that would have saved Molly from being knocked into the water. At the same time they are resenting her a little for being so wet and unhappy that they must cut short their sail and take her back to shore. As for Molly, she is simply miserable.

Carl reaches forward and pats her wet leg, awkwardly, apologetically. "Sorry you went over, Moll," he says. "Cheer up. We'll have you warm soon."

Molly looks up at him, unsmiling. "I want to go home," she says. And it is not the Connecticut house that she is talking about.

In the big kitchen Molly is huddled inside sweater and jeans, though the sun still shines brightly outdoors and Russell and his friend Jack are splashing merrily in the pool. From the baby monitor on the kitchen table she can hear small snuffling noises, as Donald, upstairs in his crib, tries to resist falling asleep. Kate is at the sink tipping a pot of green beans into a colander. Molly pulls eight hamburger buns from a plastic bag and mounds them on a tray, beside bottles of ketchup, mustard, sweet relish, and a jar of her grandmother's green tomato chutney.

"Tell me if Carl's ready to cook," says Kate, and Molly takes her tray outside to the imposing gas grill, set into a granite counter on a specially built pillar of carved stone blocks. American husbands can indeed cook, she has learned, but they only do it outdoors, on grills, in the summer. Carl is standing beside the grill with a long fork in one hand and a cell phone in the other; he is talking into the phone.

"Okay then," he says. "Fax it to me tonight. I'll check it first thing, and get back to you. But Tuesday I go to Italy for three days. Okay. *Ciao.*" He clicks the little phone shut, and smiles his eye-crinkling smile at Molly.

"Italy?" Molly says.

"Just three days," Carl says. "Want to bring me the burgers?" He takes the tray from her, and yells over her head, "Out of the water, guys! Chow time!"

By the time Carl has cooked eight glossy hamburgers and turkey burgers, replacing them on the grill with ears of corn, Russell and Jack are in shorts and T-shirts, loading their plates with potato salad and green beans. Jack is a tall, chunky, confident boy with a very short summer crew cut; his fleshy, sun-reddened neck looks like the chin of a fat man who has forgotten to shave. He helps himself to two hamburgers, and his hand hovers doubtfully over the jar of green tomato chutney. "What's this?" he demands.

"Tomato chutney," says Molly, hostile. "My granny made it."

Jack reaches for the mustard. "Tomatoes are red, kid," he says.

"Not in England," says Russell amiably. He squeezes ketchup over his hamburger bun. "It rains a lot in England. Everything stays green. I thought you said you'd been there?"

"I was young," Jack says through a mouthful. "Mostly I remember the pigeons. In that square in London with the dude on top of a pole. I remember feeding the pigeons. They pooped on everything, including the dude on the pole. They sat on his head. Pooping pigeons. Super-pooping pigeons." He snorts with laughter. So does Russell.

Kate is sitting cross-legged on the ground, eating green beans with her fingers. She says tolerantly, "You're such a poet, Jack."

"It's not a pole, it's made of stone," Molly says. "Nelson's Column." She is suddenly overcome by a great wave of homesickness. Her mind fills with Trafalgar Square and its wheeling clouds of pigeons, and Merton Square with its garden of grass and trees, and her eyes fill with tears.

"Super-poopers," says Jack, and he and Russell fall about with silly laughter.

It is the next day, and for a treat, Carl has driven his family north on the thunderous highway, weaving his way around enormous speeding trucks; an hour's drive, to Mystic Seaport. He wants to show Kate and Molly one of the showpieces of the state in which he grew up, and he and Russell love the place anyway, because it is focused on the sea.

But although the sky is blue when they leave, clouds start to close in as they drive north. It is a grey day when they arrive at Mystic. Donald, who always falls asleep in the car, is woken up and transferred from his car-seat to his stroller, and Carl shepherds his little group toward the Visitor Center. Rain begins gently to fall. Raincoat hoods are pulled up. Then suddenly the rain becomes much harder, and instinctively everyone looks around for refuge. Russell points to a café across the street.

But Molly finds herself gripped suddenly by an extraordinary wave of emotion. She stops stock-still; it is as if someone, somewhere, has urgently called her name. She looks up, and sees next to her the door of a shop. It is a bookshop, with its name painted on the glass door: SHIPS AND THE SEA—and she knows, without question or reason, that she has to go inside.

"Let's go in here!" she calls, and there is such confidence in her voice that nobody finds the urge to disagree. They join her. Molly reaches for the old-fashioned brass handle of the door and in they all go.

A small grey-haired man is sitting at a desk on the right-hand side of the shop, just inside the door. He looks up in pleased surprise at the sight of five people tumbling in, even though one of them is a baby. "Good afternoon," he says.

"Hi," says Carl. Kate smiles, and Donald gives a loud friendly squawk.

The grey-haired man pushes back his chair and stands up. He is very small indeed, Molly sees; barely as tall as she is herself. He says, "Looking for anything in particular?"

His voice sounds English, Molly notices with surprise and approval. She looks at him uncertainly. There seems nothing about him that could have given her that unsettling sense of being summoned.

Carl says, "Just browsing, I guess." He grins. "And keeping out of the rain."

"Rain is the shopkeeper's friend," says the man cheerfully.

Russell says, "Do you have books about sailboats?"

"Can a fish swim?" says the grey-haired man. He smiles at Russell to show that he is not mocking him, and he points. "History of sail is on that wall, along with steam and power-boats. Picture books on that big table. Technical books on sailing in the back room, left-hand side. Old copies of sailing magazines too." Having started this recital, he clearly decides he might as well keep going. He points in a different direction, past a large standing globe. "Oceanography over there. Marine biology. Naval history in the side room, over there on the right."

Carl and Russell drift away, peering at the shelves.

Kate says tentatively, "Any children's books, perhaps?"

"The whole right wall of the naval history room, don't ask me why," says the man. He looks more carefully at Kate. "What part of England are you from?"

Kate laughs, and moves Donald's stroller sideways just before he can grab at a rack of maps. "London," she says. "And you?"

Molly thinks: *we are all members of a secret society.*

"Portsmouth," he says. "A very long time ago. Alan Waterford, at your service."

Donald stretches out a hand for the maps, finds he can't reach them, and lets out an angry shriek. Molly squats beside his stroller to distract him, but he will not be distracted; he bellows, and tears spill from his eyes and run down his small face, which has turned bright red.

"He's hungry, I expect," Kate says. "I brought a bottle." She extracts her squalling son from the stroller and looks hesitantly at the grey-haired bookseller. "Mr. Waterford—I didn't come in here to feed my baby, but could I tuck myself discreetly in a corner for fifteen minutes?"

"Be my guest," says Mr. Waterford, and Kate carries Donald away into the naval history room. Molly turns the pages of an enormous book of photographs called *The Sea*, and is unsettled by pictures of huge angry waves, and a small boat fighting its way through a green blur of storm. She feels depressed by the prospect of spending her whole life as part of a passionately nautical family.

Russell comes wandering out of the naval history room and crosses to join his father at the technical sailing shelves. Molly goes in to join her mother. She is sitting in a corner with Donald, who is sucking at his bottle with furious concentration.

"The way to a man's heart is through his stomach," Kate says cheerfully.

Molly laughs, and moves along the shelves, which seem to be filled with accounts of battles and naval campaigns. She is not much interested in battles. But propped up against the books on one shelf she sees two small picture-frames, and in one of them there is a drawing of Nelson's Column, and the great bronze lions that guard its base.

"Oh look, Mum," she says. "Trafalgar Square." She shows Kate the picture.

Kate studies it. "No pigeons," she says.

"That Jack is a pain," says Molly. She peers at the other picture. It shows Lord Nelson dying at the Battle of Trafalgar, amongst a group of men aboard HMS *Victory*. All the books on the shelf behind it seem to be about Nelson. She stares at them. That sense of some powerful unknown emotion clutches at her again.

She puts the Trafalgar Square picture back in its place. There is a sudden crack of thunder from outside, and she jumps. Very slowly, almost of its own accord, her hand moves across the shelf to a book.

Yes, says a soundless voice in her head.

Nervously, she takes the book off the shelf. It is called *The Life of Nelson,* and is written by Robert Southey. It is an old, battered-looking book, with a faded navy-blue cover, but there is a handsome picture of Nelson inside, and Molly finds she likes it very much. She suddenly feels she absolutely must have this book.

"Mum?" she says to Kate. "Can I buy a book?"

"Depends what it costs," Kate says.

Molly looks inside *The Life of Nelson* but can see no price written there. She carries the book into the main part of the shop. Nobody is there but Mr. Waterford, back at his desk, bent over a pile of papers. Thunder is rumbling outside in a long murmur, and the day has grown dark; the lights in the shop seem much brighter now.

"Mr. Waterford?" she says. "Please, how much is this book?"

He looks up from his papers, startled, and for a moment does not see her. She has the feeling that inside his head he was a long, long way away, and is having trouble coming back. Being a reader, Molly knows such feelings well; she has often been so deep in the world of a book that she has ignored summonses back to the life of everyday, for something as boring and irrelevant as homework or lunch.

She crosses to Mr. Waterford's desk and puts the book down in front of him. Now that she is closer, she sees that he is not so very old, in spite of the grey hair—not nearly as old as her grandfather back in London. Mr. Waterford's face is not much lined; it is almost boyish, and yet somehow wise, as if he knows far more than anyone else she has ever met.

He runs a finger along the cover of the book, almost as if he were testing it in some way. Then he opens it. "Ah," he says. "Southey."

"How much does it cost, please?" Molly says.

"Are you interested in Horatio Nelson?" says Mr. Waterford. He looks over his half-glasses at her; his eyes are grey, like his hair. Odd, pale eyes.

Molly does not know how to describe her sudden passionate determination to own this book. "He reminds me of home," she says.

"Ah," says Mr. Waterford. "I understand." And she feels that he does. But he says, "This isn't the best biography, you know. There are several modern ones that are much more readable. More objective, too."

Molly will not be budged. "I like this one," she says.

"Well," says Mr. Waterford. He looks at the front pages of the book. "Eighteen hundred and ninety-seven. Heinemann edition. Twenty-five dollars."

"Oh," says Molly in dismay.

"But not in good condition," Mr. Waterford says, as if he were talking to himself. "Nor in great demand. Five dollars, I think."

"Thank you!" says Molly, brightening.

"Do you have five dollars?" Mr. Waterford asks her.

"Oh yes," says Molly. "At least, if Mum will advance me my pocket money. She will, I know she will."

"What is your name?" Mr. Waterford asks her.

"Molly. Molly Jennings."

She finds she can't stop looking at the light grey eyes; they hold her, like hands. Mr. Waterford says, "I tell you what, Molly, you can have Lord Nelson for two dollars. I think you are the right person for this book." And he hands it to her.

The wet street outside gleams white for an instant as lightning flashes in the sky above, and thunder rumbles again, but more gently. Carl and Russell emerge from some far recess, each carrying two books, and Kate comes out of the naval history room with a docile contented Donald in her arms. In her hand she has an old copy of Hardie Gramatky's *Little Toot*.

Carl pays for all the books, including Molly's. "I think I can afford that, honey," he tells her amiably. Molly wonders if the price should go back to twenty-five dollars if Carl is paying for it, and she glances enquiringly at Mr. Waterford.

But Mr. Waterford just smiles and tucks a bookmark in the book, his grey eyes hidden again now behind the glasses, and they leave his shop. Outside, the rain is falling steadily and the wind has picked up. Carl decides to postpone their exploration of Mystic Seaport's historical ships to another day. They make their way to their car. Donald falls asleep in his stroller, and wakes up only for long enough to be strapped into his car-seat, and falls asleep again.

Molly and Russell sit in the backseat beside him. Russell flips through his books as they drive, and then looks curiously at Molly.

"Everything okay?" he says.

"Uh," Molly says. "I might have gone sideways for a bit. But yes, I'm okay." And in a little while she too falls asleep, with her *Life of Nelson* on her lap, and she dreams a dream that she does not remember afterward, just as most of us do not remember many of our dreams.

SAM

JANUARY 1803

I NEVER HAD ANY THOUGHT OF JOINING THE NAVY, UNTIL
AFTER THAT DAY MY UNCLE CAME.

I was eleven years old, though I looked older, being tall and
sturdy for my age. The Lord knows why that should have been
so; we never had enough to eat. There were five of us children.
All our lives we had lived in a cottage on the lands of the great
house, Lord Melcher's house. In Kent, that was, in the green
countryside. My father labored there. He went every day to
plow or cut hay or whatever the bailiff wanted, according to
season, and my mother worked sometimes in the kitchen at the
great house, washing pots. Mostly though, she worked in our

home for his lordship's housekeeper, sewing, because she was good with her needle and could mend fine clothes or work with linens. When I see her in my mind, she is bent close over her sewing, beside the dim little lamp, peering to see the stitches.

The walls of our cottage were made of wattle and daub, thick enough to keep out the wind, and the roof was of thatch, and leaked. Often my brother and I had to climb up on the thatch and stuff hay into a place where we thought the leak might be. For the seven in our family there were two rooms, one at the front for cooking and eating and the other for sleep-ing. The front room had the hearth, so between the two rooms there was only half a wall, to let the heat go through. All of us slept there in the back on straw mattresses, in a row: me on the end, then my three little sisters Mary, Alice and Beth, then Mam, my father and my big brother Dick.

I took Mary and Alice to school in spring and autumn, but Beth was too young, only a baby. There was another baby to come soon; my mother's belly was swelling again. My father was always turning to her at night, whether she wanted it or not. He would start to snore as soon as he was done. Once, afterward, I reached out across my little sisters' heads to stroke Mam's hair just for a moment, and she kissed my hand and I could feel that her cheek was wet.

I hated my father. He was all shouting and hitting; there was never a kind word out of him. He worked hard, but that was the most you could say for him, in my opinion. My elder brother Dick was the same, always picking fights with me because he knew he could win. Our tiny humpbacked schoolteacher Mr. Jenkin was worth five of them, though Dick would have thrashed me if I had told him so. Mr. Jenkin said I was the best reader he had ever had, but my only sight of school now was in taking the little girls. My father said I had had more than enough schooling, and wanted me always out digging or getting firewood.

Soon he would have me off with him and Dick to be a laborer on the farm. I was there often already, helping with the hens and the sheep, but this was a good year for catching rabbits and my father knew I was skillful at that. So he gave me time for my snares, and I skinned the rabbits and fixed the skins to a board and rubbed ashes into them, and if they were any good Mam would make us a jerkin or a hat. The most important thing was the meat; she made a stew whenever I caught a rabbit. My father and Dick always ate most of it.

It was winter when my uncle came. Winter was the worst time, always wet and cold. However much straw we laid on the earth floor of the cottage, water came in under the door and turned the earth to mud; it was almost better when the ground froze. My mother kept a fire burning in the hearth for as much of those short days as she could manage, but you had to be close to it to be even half warm. She made broth to warm us up, if my father brought home a carrot or turnip or two from the fields. On the day I am telling you about, Dick brought home a slab of bacon that one of the cooks at the big house had given him when he delivered a sack of potatoes. She thought him a likely fellow, I dare say; girls did, sometimes. They didn't know him the way I did.

"Good lad!" my father said, when he smelled the bacon and

heard where it came from. "That's the kind of son to have, not one that sits sewing like a girl."

He meant me. Mam was hemming sheets for the big house, and it was a lot of work so I was helping her. She'd taught me how to sew when I was a little fellow, wanting to copy whatever she did.

"The sewing pays money," my mother said.

My father gave a scornful snort, and let go a great fart for good measure. He took the best seat by the fire, and Beth came climbing into his lap, not out of affection but because it was the only place to be warm.

Then there was a man's voice calling outside, and the door opened, and in out of the cold rain came the dripping figure of my uncle.

I didn't know who he was, but my mother let out the most joyful cry I had ever heard in my life.

"Charlie!"

She ran to him and flung her arms round him, wet jacket and all, and they stood hugging each other for a long minute while we children gaped, and my father sat unmoving by the fire.

My mother and my uncle Charlie were brother and sister, you see. They had grown up together very close, in their big family in the town of Chatham, on the coast. But somehow my mother met my father and married him, and he took her away from Chatham to our cottage. Until this day, Mam told us, she hadn't seen her brother Charlie for thirteen years. Certainly none of us had ever seen him before—though we knew about him from the stories Mam had always told us about her family, faraway people, separated from us by limitless time and space.

Suddenly now one of them was real. I stared at him. He was a short, stocky man, with broad powerful shoulders and a cheerful kind of face. Like Mam and me, he had blue eyes and straight light brown hair.

Mam told him all our names, and he nodded to each one of us, and smiled. Then Mam took the pot off the fire, and divided the soup between eight dishes instead of seven. She took a very small one for herself. I could see my father keeping a sharp eye on how much bacon went into his own dish, and Dick's, and Charlie's: I knew Mam had cut off and saved most of the fat bacon to use later, so only the meaty bits, which we hardly ever saw, were in the pot with the broth and potatoes.

Uncle Charlie said, "Just a touch of broth for me, Em—I'm not hungry."

"Rubbish!" said my mother. "You always ate three times as much as me."

"Not tonight," he said, "I ate on the road."

I knew how good the broth smelled, and I knew how far away the traveling road was, so that was when I knew I liked my uncle.

We ate our supper. There was bread, our heavy stale bread, so Uncle Charlie ate a small chunk of it deliberately slowly, and I liked him even more. He and my mother talked about family, and the girls and I listened greedily, trying to put it all in our memories. My father and Dick ate, bored.

Then my father said, "Why have you come here?"

Uncle Charlie looked at him, considering. For a moment I saw a look of my mother in his face.

He said, "There was a wagon coming this way, and going back again. I wanted to see my sister. And perhaps to help."

"Help?" said my father. He spat into the fire. "Who says we need help?"

"There are five children," my uncle said mildly. "And one more on the way, I see."

"And two that died," my mother said. Uncle Charlie reached out and touched her hand, very quickly, just for a moment. He said, "I am a spinner at the ropewalk in Chatham. The Navy has great need of rope, in all these years of war. I do well. My wife and I had but one child, and he died young. I could take one of your boys and start him at the ropewalk too, if you want. It is hard, but a living."

Dick was sitting on a hunk of wood beside my father. He looked up eagerly. "Me!" he said. "I want to go!"

My father swung his arm across quick as light and hit Dick with the back of his hand, knocking him sideways. "Speak when you're asked!" he said.

Dick wiped a little blood off his mouth. We were all used to being hit. He said, low, "I'm the biggest. I'm strong."

"So you stay here," my father said. "I'm not giving you up—the bailey likes you." He looked over at me, and suddenly I felt my mother's hand on my shoulder, light, quivering.

"You could take that one," my father said to Charlie, jerking his head at me. His eyes narrowed, and you could almost see his piggy little brain working. "What do I get for losing him?"

"Whatever he earns, until he's grown," said my uncle. "Joan and I will house him."

"Take him," my father said. "He eats more than he gets."

My mother's fingers tightened on my shoulder, and I heard her make a little lost sound, like a baby makes.

My uncle looked at me. "Will you come, Sam?"

I was giddy at the thought of getting away from my father. I had never imagined there could be any escape. But I felt the hand on my shoulder, trembling now. I turned my head and looked at my mother, at her poor tired face. There was a tear running down from each eye, but she firmed her mouth and nodded her head.

"All right," I said to my uncle.

He said slowly, with his eyes on my mother, "We must leave at first light—the wagon will be by."

"Sam will be ready," she said. And at this the little girls set up a great squalling, and my father shouted at them, and threw his empty bowl to the floor in a fury.

But when dawn came, my life changed. My mother hugged me to her so tightly, before my uncle and I set out for the road and the world beyond. I shall remember that hugging till the day I die.

For just five days I thought I was in heaven. The wagon creaked and bumped and splashed its way along the road to Chatham, with Uncle Charlie and me tucked in beside a great load of cabbages and squawking chickens, and after half a day I began to see a thousand things I had never seen before. Tall red-brown buildings of brick rose all around us, houses and shops and such, and a press of carts and carriages. Once, a grand stagecoach came spanking along behind six galloping horses, with a man blowing a long horn like the Last Trump in the Bible. As we came into the city, the streets were made of lumpy stones called cobbles, and full of more people than I had ever known existed in the world. All was noise, shouting voices and creaking wheels; everywhere people were selling and buying, calling out to others about their fruit or fish or wool. Our wagon slowed down near a young woman with a great armful of red and white roses for sale. She grinned up at me, a gap-toothed grin, and she yelled, "Throw us a cabbage, my duck!"

I did, too, just a little one. She tossed me a red rose, but it fell in the street.

In my uncle's house there was a floor of wood, and a stairway leading up to another floor. We ate meat, twice in less than a week, and I slept on my own mattress, in a little room with nobody else in it. My aunt Joan was a chubby lady with smiling lines on her face, and she fed me as if every day were Christmas. The first evening, I kept finding her gazing at me with a wondering expression on her face. After a while I caught her eye so often that she burst out laughing.

"Forgive me, Sam," she said. "I stare at your face because you are so much like your uncle. It is like meeting Charlie all over again, when we were young."

"So you better keep clear of my wife, lad," said my uncle, smiling. He took hold of my chin and studied my face for a moment. The smile faded, and he shook his head rather sadly. "I see my sister, days long gone," he said.

I think that was the first time I had the feeling, like a quick pain, that life goes by terribly fast.

On the fifth day, my uncle took me with him to the ropewalk. Chatham Dockyard was a huge, amazing place. We walked through the streets for a long time to get there, through a warren of buildings that made me feel squashed just by looking at them. My uncle quickened his pace, and more men came hurrying all around us, all headed the same way. I began to hear a deep bell ringing, slowly at first, then gradually faster, and all the hurrying men began to run toward a high wall, thronging through tall open gates.

"The muster bell!" my uncle called to me as I ran to keep up. It meant, I found afterward, that if you wanted a full day's pay you had to be at work before that bell stopped ringing.

Ahead of us was the ropewalk, a long wooden building, and beyond it I could see the sky full of the masts and rigging of the ships in the dockyard.

When my uncle led me in through the doors in the middle of the ropewalk I stopped dead still in astonishment. It was full of a deafening rattling noise, and the musty smell of hemp, but the most overwhelming thing was just its length. In both directions the walls, and the wooden rails that carried the rope-making machines, stretched so far that you couldn't see where they ended. It was like standing on a long, long straight road that runs to the horizon. The whole building was a quarter of a mile long, so that they could make the standard length of ropes needed for ships: one hundred fathoms. A fathom is six feet; it's the way sailors measure the depth of the ocean. I didn't know that then.

There was a huge amount I didn't know then, from having spent my whole life in the country. I learned a lot even that first day, from listening to my uncle and his friends. Everyone was expecting England to go to war with France and its ally Spain, because Napoleon Bonaparte was planning to take over all of

Europe. He already had quite a lot of it. Until last year, said my uncle, we had been fighting France for years, mostly at sea. Pretty soon it would all start again, and our Royal Navy would have to fight off the navies of France and Spain and stop Bonaparte from invading the British Isles. At every shipyard in Britain, ships were being built at a frenzied rate, and since the rigging of a big battleship used *twenty-seven miles* of rope, besides heavy anchor cables and such, the ropewalks everywhere were also in a frenzy.

I watched my uncle getting ready for work, on the upper level of the ropewalk, and I was in awe of him. He was a spinner, and he was like a little king. Because I was his nephew, all the men in his team greeted me kindly, even the man in charge of them all, that they called the gaffer. I can't tell you how happy I was that day; I had never known anything like it. My uncle's apprentice, a tall, lean, young man called Will, even took time to explain the rope-making to me. He said the raw hemp came to the dockyard from Russia, in great bales like hay, and first it was soaked in whale oil to make it more supple, and then pulled through boards with metal spikes sticking up out of them, to make the fibers all lie in one direction. The men who did this were called hatchellers and they seemed to be pretty important too, but not like my uncle. Not like the spinners.

Have you ever watched anyone spinning wool? I had, on the farm; it's like magic, the way all those separate strands off the sheep's back are twisted together into one long thread. My uncle Charlie and the other spinners worked this same magic with hemp. There were four of them spinning at any one time, two at one end of the long long walk and two at the other. Each one had a bundle of hemp wrapped round his waist, its end attached to three hooks on a round frame that another man turned with a handle—and as the frame turned, the spinner walked backward, spinning those hemp fibers into yarn with his hands. It was the beginning of all rope; three strands made from that yarn would be turned into most of the rigging of a ship.

My uncle began his backward spinning walk, and the wheel frame rattled as it turned round. He glanced up and grinned at me as he backed past me, hands turning. I watched him disappear down the long walk. I wanted passionately to learn how to do what he did, one day.

Then the young man Will was upon me—"Your time for work, Samuel!"—and he set me to sweeping up loose hemp all along the ropewalk, with a broom almost as big as me. That was what I did all day, because ropewalks have to be kept clean, safe from the danger of fire. Sweep, sweep, sweep; before I was a tenth of the way down the walk I had blisters on the palms of both hands. I tried to shift the broom to different places in my hands to avoid the blisters, and kept sweeping.

Somewhere in the middle of the day we paused, for just long enough to eat the packages of bread and cheese that Aunt Joan had given us at dawn. We sat outdoors on bales of hemp, my uncle and me and the other men in his team. It was a cold day but sunny, and a release from the sweaty heat inside the ropewalk. The machines clattered on in there; when a few men were given a break, others took over, so that the work should never stop.

I listened to the men talking about the war, in wonderment at all the things taking place beyond my cottage childhood. I wished I could report it all to my schoolmaster Mr. Jenkin. The men were fiercely proud of Chatham Dockyard, and of all the ships built there. The biggest of these was HMS *Victory*, which had been built forty years ago and had just been back in the dockyard for a long refit. Every inch of her rigging had come from this ropewalk, and a lot of it spun by my uncle. Three other ships were under refit in the dry docks now. Theirs were the masts I could see beyond the end of the long ropewalk. I liked the smell of the sea, and the wild calls of the seagulls wheeling overhead.

"Keep up the sweeping, young Sam," said Will, as we went back up the narrow wooden stairs to the spinning walk. "The gaffer will take you on, I reckon. I saw his eye on you."

"Good!" said my uncle. Since the gaffer was the master of that part of the ropewalk, he did the hiring.

"I got blisters," I said proudly, and showed them.

"You'll toughen up," my uncle said. "Like this." He held out his hands to me. I hadn't noticed before, but his palms and fingers were calloused thick as leather, from years of pulling the raw hemp into a yarn.

I said, "I want to be a spinner."

They all laughed. "Very well," said my uncle's partner Henry, a grizzled old man with a big belly. "Just get yourself stronger, boy. Watch your uncle at the start of a run—that's sixty-five pounds of hemp round his waist to be carried and fingered into yarn, and he does that eighteen times a day."

And I did watch, as I swept, and marveled at how hard the work was, in this town just as in the country. But here, I could earn money, and send it somehow to my mother.

I was triple blistered, and very tired, when the workday ended and the night shift came on—the ropewalk never stopped in this time of war and shipbuilding. But the gaffer said that I could stay, so I was happy as I stumbled along with my uncle and Will through the dark streets, past glowing doorways with voices shouting and singing inside. Those were taverns, I guessed, where men got drunk. I had heard my father talk of them, with an anger that might have been envy.

It was noise from a tavern, as we turned a corner, that drowned out the sound of a brawl ahead of us in the street, and the cries of warning. "Run! Run! They'll take you! Run!" We heard the voices, but too late.

And suddenly hands seized us, and I saw my uncle twist angrily and strike out, and then fall as a man hit him with a kind of short club. I shrieked and tried to reach him, and that's all I remember. Someone must have hit me too, and I was out.

I woke up, dazed, to find myself hanging head down, swinging and bumping to and fro, over the shoulder of a huge evil-smelling lout in a crowd of shouting men. There were dozens of them, and they were dragging the poor wretches they had caught along the dark street. Women were screaming curses at them from bright doorways, and some were throwing things, or beating at them with any weapon they could find, a rolling pin or a chair leg. I caught quick glimpses, as the world swung round my upside-down eyes. I had no idea what was happening to me. I tried to kick at the back of my captor, and he grunted in anger and punched my head, so that my teeth bit my tongue. Blood came salt in my mouth, and it hurt so much that I went limp and hung helpless, rather than anger him again.

I knew they must have caught Uncle Charlie and Will too, but I could see nothing but a blur of bodies.

There must have been about thirty of us. They took us to a house where two flaming torches were fixed over the doorway. The giant holding me swung me down onto my feet, and pushed me with the rest into a room crammed with other captured men, all yelling and cursing and pleading as the door opened. And when we were inside, the door closed again. I was terrified. The man pressed nearest to me smelled like a tavern, and his eyes were rolling in his head. Gradually the eyes fixed themselves on my face, and he gave me a horrible sly smile.

"Aren't you a pretty boy?" he said, and he groped his hand out at me—and then doubled over shrieking, as someone's knee smashed into his gut.

It was my uncle, with Will beside him. Men drew back, making a little space around us. Will kicked at the drunk, and he vomited on the floor.

"Scum!" my uncle said. His face was tight with anger and worry.

I clutched his arm. I could hear my voice come out high, like a tiny boy's. "What's happening? What are they going to do to us?"

"It is the Navy," my uncle said. "When they need sailors, they take men from the streets—it is called being pressed into service."

"Every lad's nightmare," said Will bitterly. "Being caught by the Press!"

The door swung open again, and three soldiers in uniform

hauled out half a dozen of the nearest men—and we were amongst them.

"March—this way—come on, you dogs—" and we were in a brightly lit room arrayed with four more soldiers, with guns this time. They were the soldiers of the Navy, called marines, but I didn't know that then. They were standing along the wall, behind a table, and at the table sat a naval officer, a fat young man with a pink face. He wore a beautiful uniform, a dark blue coat with white cuffs and gleaming gold buttons, and white breeches. On the table in front of him was a black cocked hat, and beside it a lamp and a big open book.

"Next," he said, and pointed at my uncle, who was thrust forward by the butt of a marine's gun before he had a chance to move by himself. He stumbled, and stood there scowling.

"Name," said the officer, barely looking at him. He dipped a pen in an inkpot.

"I am Charles Davis of Chatham and I work at the dockyard," my uncle said. "I am a spinner in the ropewalk, we are exempt from the Press."

"A likely tale," said the fat young officer. "Let's look at your hands."

My uncle spread his calloused palms. "A spinner's hands," he said.

The officer snorted. "Those are the hands of every jack in the Navy, my friend. You're a merchant seaman." He wrote in his book. "Age?"

"Thirty-six," my uncle said. His voice was tight and tense, I could feel him forcing himself not to shout. "And I am no seaman, sir."

"But now you have the opportunity to serve in His Majesty's Navy," said the officer, writing. "You are a fortunate fellow. Next."

He turned his head to me.

My uncle started talking in a rush, resisting the marine who was trying to drag him away. "Sir," he said, "this is my nephew, who is not but eleven years of age. He is a child. In all humanity I ask you to let him go."

The pink-cheeked young man surveyed me and then my struggling uncle. "Stuff," he said. "Look at the size of him, he is at least fourteen years old. Are you not, boy?"

I said huskily, "I am eleven, sir."

"Ill-educated in numbers, I see," he said blandly. "Name?"

"Samuel Robbins, sir."

"Where are you from?"

"Hunter Green," I said. "A village north of here."

"Oh la," he said, writing. "Let us set down London. Go with these fine marines, you and your uncle, and you will have excitement and adventures, and money in your pocket the rest of your days."

I said, because I had not thought of it, "Money?"

"Seven pounds a year for a boy," the officer said. He smiled to himself, perhaps at the difference between that and his own pay.

"Shall I be able to send it to my mother?"

"Of course!" he said.

My uncle tried again. "Sir, have pity on—"

"Enough!" said the officer sharply, and thumped the table. The flame of the lamp flickered wildly. And the marines pulled us out of the room, as he turned his attention to Will.

It was Will, as things turned out, who was the only one of us to escape being pressed. I remember that night only as a blur of noise and shoving and stumbling, with my wits still fuzzled by the blow on my head. But I know that maybe twenty of us, out of the crowd in that first room of pressed men, were taken through the streets to the River Medway, upstream from the dockyard, and hustled down a flight of slippery stone steps to a jetty, and then into a broad open boat. Some of the men had irons on their legs or arms, but the press gang had run through their stock of irons just as Will, my uncle and I were brought down, and so we were not chained.

It was dark. The water was very black and it smelled dank, like a ditch. We were pushed down into the boat, to sit there in a huddle between the sailors taking their places at twelve big oars. A wind was picking up, and small waves smacked at the sides of the boat. The tossing was strange to me, for I had never been in a boat before in my life. We were pushed off from the jetty, and the boat lurched to and fro as the sailors raised their oars and waited for the order to row. There was a lantern swaying over the back of the boat, but we were in the front, in shadow. Will was near me; I noticed he took care to press himself against the side of the boat, well ahead of the first oarsman.

Suddenly my uncle gave a great shriek from the other side of the mass of chained men. "A rat!" he howled. "I am bitten! There are rats in this boat!"

There was a hubbub at once. Everyone fears rats. The other men began to shout and shift about. "Rats!" they cried. "Beware the rats!"

The boat tossed from side to side, even though it was a

broad, heavy thing, and the officer in charge shouted angrily. The marines in the boat thumped out at the men with their gun-stocks to keep them still—though I noticed that even they peered warily round the bottom of the boat as they did so. In a while, there was a command—"Oars—ready—row!" The sea-men began to pull, and gradually we moved out into the middle of the river, heading for the estuary where the great ships were at anchor.

Will was no longer beside me. It was too dark for me to see where he had gone, so I curled myself into an unhappy lump on the bottom of the boat, and thought about my mother, and tried not to cry. I found out later that Will was no longer in the boat at all. In the moments while everyone was distracted by my uncle's shriek, he had slipped over the side into the water. My uncle told me afterward that they had planned it together, whis-pering hastily in the only few minutes they could snatch. Unlike the rest of us, he said, Will could swim like an eel. He was the son of a fisherman and had grown up on and in the water every summer. He knew that if he had just an instant's chance to get into the sea, he could dive down and swim silently away below the surface. So my uncle gave him his chance.

The water was choppier as we headed out into the estuary. I grew more and more miserable as the boat tossed, and I felt sick. Before long I threw up in the bottom of the boat, and made my poor neighbors miserable too. I lay there curled up in a ball with my eyes shut, feeling gobs of seawater splash over me, and I clutched my arms round my shoulders and cried like a baby. I didn't care who heard me. I wanted my mother, I wanted her arms round me, I wanted to be at home.

By the time we reached the towering side of a great ship I could neither see nor hear what was happening, what with the rising and falling of our boat, which now seemed so small, and an enormous eerie sound overhead that was the whistling of the wind in the ropes of the ship's rigging. One by one we were sent up the huge side of the ship, clinging to a kind of rope ladder; it was hard to catch hold of it from the tossing boat, and I would have fallen into the sea if my uncle had not been close behind me, helping.

And once up on the deck of the ship there was no relief, nor any care for us, for we were herded down a narrow stairway into a miserable space where we were shut behind a grating, with about a dozen others who were there already. There they left us all night, with only a leather bucket of water and a panikin to share it with, and a basket of what was called bread but was biscuit hard as wood. If they counted us they must have noticed one was missing, which meant trouble for someone in charge. I hope it was the fat young officer, though I never saw him again.

My uncle said to the sailor who locked us in, "What ship is this?"

The man stared, then laughed. "Damme, what loons have they sent us? This is Captain Sutton's ship, cully—HMS Victory."

Molly

2006

MOLLY IS CRYING. VERY QUIETLY, SO THAT NOBODY SHALL HEAR HER. THE TEARS RUN DOWN HER CHEEKS AND DRIP FROM the sides of her chin, and once in a while she blows her nose. But she goes on crying. They are tears of hopelessness, shed for something that she knows she cannot change.

She is homesick. She sits hunched on the window-seat of her pretty bedroom, specially decorated for her by Carl (not with his own hands, but on his orders) before she arrived. Its walls are pale yellow and its many bookshelves are white; it has a white wicker armchair and a beautiful ash-wood desk, and a roomy bed with a flowered quilt. On the two bedside tables are two lamps, their shades perched over the cheerful papier-mâché shapes of a high-collared Victorian gentleman and his demure wife. It is a picture-book room, much larger and more comfortable than her room in the London flat, and she is crying because she wants to leave it and cannot. She wants to go home, but home is no longer there, even though it is not here either.

She misses England. She misses the grey streets and green parks of London; she misses her friends, and the neighbors who were so familiar even though they exchanged no more than a faint smile each day. She misses Grandad and Granny, and the red double-decker buses, and even her school uniform. She is overwhelmed by America, where everything seems bigger and louder and more confident, and she is terrified by the prospect of being launched into the seventh grade at the enormous local school in a month's time. Part of the terror is due to the fact that Molly is epileptic.

It is a very mild kind of epilepsy, an occasional short-circuiting in the brain, and she has had no symptoms for so long that the doctor thinks she has grown out of it. Molly is a perfectly normal girl, physically and mentally, but she knows that there have been times, now and again, when she has seemed to lose track of what is going on around her. Sally, her best friend, used to describe it as "going sideways." She said once, "You get that vague look in your eyes. I can always tell—you don't hear what I'm saying, you're like some whizzbang genius solving a problem in her head. Only you aren't a genius, you're just old Moll going sideways."

Molly smiles at the remembered voice. She blows her nose, and decides to write Sally an e-mail. What will she do without

Sally, and her other friends Jen and Naomi, when she is alone at this huge new school? Who will look out for her, and understand, if her face becomes vacant for a few minutes? They will all think she's crazy, or a complete geek.

She scrambles down from the window-seat, tosses several wet tissues into the wastepaper basket, and goes out into her little bathroom to splash water on her face. Here in Carl's Connecticut house she has her very own bathroom, all white and yellow to match the bedroom, with a print of van Gogh's sunflowers on the wall. It is somehow part of the same pattern as the big two-acre garden, with its swimming pool and tennis court; it's too much, she doesn't belong there. Though when she had described it to Sally, disparagingly, Sally had e-mailed back that she thought Molly must have died and gone to heaven.

"Hey, Moll? Kate says there's tea if you want it." Russell is passing the open door of the bathroom. He thunders down the stairs, yelling "Hey, lunkhead!" at someone below, and Molly realizes with a sinking feeling that his friend Jack must be there again. Jack's universe has no space for a much younger girl, except as an object for heavy-handed teasing. And she just plain doesn't like Jack. Seeking some symbol of self-protection, she goes back into the bedroom and snatches up a couple of books.

The prospect of teatime counterbalances the thought of Jack, so she goes downstairs to the kitchen, where the two boys are sitting on stools at the island counter drinking milk and wolfing chocolate chip cookies. Carl is not here; he has gone to Italy. Kate smiles at Molly. Without asking, she pours her a cup of tea and cuts her a piece of cake. It's a very English cake: a fluffy sponge cake with raspberry jam sandwiched in the middle, and the top sprinkled with fine granular sugar. This kind of sugar is not sold in the United States, so Kate makes it by whirling regular sugar in her blender. For Molly.

"Thanks, Mum." Molly pours milk into her tea.

"Let's have a naice cup of tea," says Jack, in an exaggerated parody of an English voice.

"You'll never make the school play, Jack," Kate says equably, though Molly knows she despises fake English accents.

"It's teataime," says Jack, undeterred. He takes another cookie and grins at Kate. "You make *delicious* bickies, Mrs. Hibbert! Just soopah!"

Kate appalls Molly by laughing at him. But Russell has noticed the expression on Molly's face. He digs his elbow into Jack's side. "Shut up, lunkhead."

Jack digs him in return, more forcibly. "What's up with you, *old chap*? Two years over there did a number on you—you should have heard your Limey accent when you came back!"

"We don't have an accent," Molly says flatly. "You do. It's our language. It's called English."

Jack crows with laughter. "Lah-di-dah!" he cries. "Lah-di-dah!" He slides off his stool and stands there, tall and chunky, mocking.

Russell gets up hastily and heads for the door. "C'mon, Yank," he says. "Time for a sail. Want to come, Molly?"

"No!" Molly says.

Kate looks at her.

Molly says reluctantly, "No, thanks."

"Seven o'clock supper," Kate says to Russell. "But not for

the All-American as well, I'm afraid—I only have three lamb chops. Sorry, Jack."

Jack turns back to grin at her. He's wearing jeans and a tank top, and his sun-reddened shoulders look enormous; he is on the high school football team, and proud of it. He leers at Kate flirtatiously, and this time he tries a terrible imitation of a Cockney accent. "Ooh, y're an 'ard-'earted woman—" he starts.

And Molly snaps.

"Stop it!" she shrieks, and she flings one of her books at him. "Just stop it!"

The book narrowly misses Jack's head and hits the wall. He blinks, startled.

Molly bursts into violent tears.

"Moll—" Russell says unhappily, starting toward her, but Kate puts an arm round Molly and waves him away.

"It's okay," she says. "Go off and sail. She'll be all right."

Jack says in confusion, "I'm sorry. I didn't mean—"

"It's okay," Kate says again. Now she has both arms round Molly, who is sobbing into her shoulder. "It's not about you. Don't worry."

Russell picks up the fallen book and puts it on the kitchen table, and the two boys go silently out of the kitchen like two big obedient baffled dogs.

All Molly's deep unhappiness has erupted out of her, like lava shooting out of a volcano. She is clutching her mother, shaken by great gut-wrenching sobs, making noises she has never in her life made before. She can't stop. Kate lets her go on for a long time, holding her close, stroking her hair, but then she starts to soothe her, crooning to her as if she were a baby: "There, love, there . . ."

Gradually Molly stops making the terrible deep noises and is merely crying. She raises her head; her face is all wet with tears and snot. "I want to go home," she weeps. "Oh Mum, I want to go home."

Kate hands her a fistful of tissues. Molly blows her nose several times. They both know that what she wants is impossible.

Kate says soberly, "Maybe I should never have married Carl."

"Oh no," Molly says. "No. It's not Carl. It's just—"

"I know," Kate says. She pulls another tissue from the box, and dries Molly's cheek. "We've turned your life upside-down. Nothing will ever be the same as it was."

A small husky sound comes from the baby monitor on the counter. It is Donald, upstairs, waking from his nap.

Kate ignores it. She puts an arm across Molly's shoulders, more lightly now. "I can remember crying like that," she says. "Twice. Once, right after your father died. Then after that I had to concentrate on being a mum for you, comforting my little four-year-old who'd lost her Daddy, so for months I hung on and tried not to cry at all. But one night when I was going to bed I remembered it was our wedding anniversary, and I fell apart, I just howled, for half the night. I cried until there were no more tears in me. Because he was gone, gone, and he would never ever come back. Nothing would ever be the same again."

Molly clutches her hand, silently.

The sounds from the baby monitor become a recognizable voice, complaining, insistent.

"Come on," says Kate. "He's hungry."

"He's always hungry," Molly says, and they go upstairs. Donald crows with pleasure at the sight of Molly, wriggling about like a happy eel as she changes his diaper. Then he catches sight of Kate and bellows with hunger.

Molly hovers, while Kate settles into the rocking chair to give him his bottle. The room is full of sunshine, with brightly colored alphabets running in a high border round the walls. Molly sits down on the floor. "Mum," she says, "when Daddy died—I know it was a plane crash, but nobody ever talks about it. What happened?"

Her mother looks down at her, across Donald's small contented head. "It was one of those accidents that never get solved," she says. "His newspaper had sent him to cover a story in North Africa, and he was on his way home. It was a normal commercial flight, but they hit bad weather and something went horribly wrong—nobody ever knew what, because they never found the plane's black box that records all the details."

Molly says, "Was it terrorists?"

"No. Not back then. It was an accident. Bad luck. Terrible luck for all the hundred and twenty-eight people on board— and all their families, like us. The plane fell into the sea just off the coast of Spain."

Molly's head whirls for a moment. *"Into the sea?"*

"You knew that," Kate says.

"No I didn't!" In her head Molly is back in the ocean after her fall from Carl's boat, spluttering in the water.

"Well . . . yes. Into the sea. But they didn't have time to drown, they must all have been killed instantly by the fall."

There is strain on Kate's face; she is not enjoying the remembering. Molly suddenly feels amazingly tired.

"I have such a headache," she says.

Kate's face changes and becomes familiar again; it is full of concern, and then understanding. "You've had quite a day, my love," she says. "Here, give me a kiss. Then go and lie down for a bit."

So Molly does. She lies on her bed thinking about an airplane falling into the sea, and then knows nothing until much later, when Kate wakes her up with a bowl of soup and a slice of apple pie, all on a tray as if she were an invalid. She has slept right through supper. She eats her soup and pie and is still tired, so she puts on her pajamas and brushes her teeth.

Russell comes up the stairs just as she is heading back into her bedroom. "Hi, Moll," he says. "Here's your book."

He hands her the faded navy-blue *Life of Nelson,* which now looks much more battered than before. "Thanks," Molly says. She sits down on her bed holding the book, looking down at its cover.

Russell is hovering in the doorway. He says awkwardly, "I'm sorry about Jack. He shoots his mouth off. But I've known him since we were little kids, y'know?"

Molly says, "I can't believe I threw a *book.*"

Russell grins. "Good thing you're a lousy shot."

Their two years of learning to be brother and sister are rescuing them. The awkwardness goes out of the air. Looking at her book, Molly can see that it has suffered greatly from becoming a missile; its binding is split, and when she opens the front cover it hangs loose, no longer joined to the rest of the book.

But there is something else there that she has not seen before.

"See you tomorrow," Russell says. He turns to go.

Molly hasn't heard him. "Look at this," she says, peering.

A new note in her voice makes Russell come into the room and look down over her shoulder. Inside the dangling front cover of *The Life of Nelson* is a piece of heavy paper which must always have been stuck to it, but which is now coming loose, and they can see that something is hidden underneath it. Molly sticks her finger underneath the edge of the paper, and it starts to tear.

"Wait a minute," Russell says. "Use this." He takes a penknife out of his pocket, opens the blade and hands it to her. Molly slips the blade under the page, and pushes it gently sideways. The ancient glue crackles and parts as the blade slides along, and the paper comes loose. At the back edge, it is still attached; they see that although it had been glued to the inside cover, it is the original first page of the book. And facing it, still stuck to the cover, is some brown paper folded over into a kind of loose envelope.

Molly touches the brown paper with one finger, but does not open it. She peers at the cover. "There's writing," she says.

Russell looks down at it, mildly interested. Below the folded paper there are some lines written on the cover in bold sprawling handwriting. Molly reads them aloud, slowly.

"*This fragment of the great man's life and death passed on to me by my grandmother at her death in eighteen eighty-nine,*" she reads. She stops.

"Go on," Russell says.

"That's all. Then a name, the man who wrote it, I suppose. Edward Austen."

"'Fragment of the great man's life and death'?" Russell says. "Weird. What's in that little wrapper?"

"The great man must be Lord Nelson," Molly says. She looks at the folded brown paper, and is nervous of touching it. She feels suddenly that she is on the edge of some huge powerful thing or happening, though she cannot imagine what. But she knows that she has to investigate, or Russell's inquiring hand will come down and do it for her. So she puts out a finger and lifts up the top flap.

Inside the roughly made envelope is a small piece of coarse, frayed cloth. It is a dirty cream color, a lighter brown than the paper around it: a ragged little piece of material about three inches square. Molly takes it out between her finger and thumb and puts it on the palm of her left hand.

And in that instant, the presence of power floods all around and through her like a great noise, so that she feels suddenly giddy. She puts her other hand flat on the bed beside her, to prop herself up. She is not frightened, not at all; it is more like an excitement, like the feeling of having been given some wonderful piece of news.

Then it is gone, as if a huge chord of music had suddenly boomed out, and then just as suddenly stopped.

Russell is gazing nervously at her face. "Moll? You look like . . . are you going to have one of your sideways times?"

"No!" Molly says. "I'm fine." She holds her palm out to him. "Look—it's a piece of cloth. It's really old."

"Yeah," Russell says, glancing at it. He is still keeping a cautious eye on her face.

Molly moves her hand to slide the little square of cloth back into its folded paper covering, but as she does so, she notices some words written on the paper itself. She pauses and instead opens out the fold.

This writing is very faint, and in a different hand: a beautiful slanting copperplate handwriting, from another age. Molly knows at once that it is much older than the inscription by Mr. Edward Austen. She has seen writing like this before, on a school visit to the British Museum in London. That day, most of the kids had obsessed over a prehistoric mummified little man, but her favorite thing had been the old handwritten letters and manuscripts, in glass-topped cases covered with velvet curtains to keep the light from fading the ink.

She starts to read aloud again. *"Thif the moft—"* then she smiles, remembering the way the old manuscripts had every *S* written like an *F*.

She reads: *"This the most precious possession of my father Samuel Robbins, his piece of the flag of HMS Victory on which he served as a boy at Trafalgar. Given into my safekeeping as a girl, before his last voyage from which he did not return. May God bless my dear father and his Admiral."*

Molly finds her voice shaking, and she stops. "Oh my goodness," she says. She stares at the piece of darkened cloth in her hand.

Russell picks up the wounded book and studies the handwriting. "There's a signature here too," he says. "Emma . . . Tenney. See?" He hands it to Molly. She looks, and nods.

"Cool," Russell says. "You got a piece of history, Moll." And Molly realizes that he has no idea of the nature of this amazing thing that has come into her life. For Russell, this is just an old book with some writing and a dubious relic in it. Though he lived for two years in England, he has come home and changed back into an American boy, and the name Nelson is no more than a memory of that dude on the pole in Trafalgar Square. If the piece of flag had something to do with George Washington, it might have kept his attention. But it is as English as Molly and her book, and besides, Russell has far more interest in sailing, girls and his impending driving test than in history.

Molly slips the square of cloth back into its brown paper covering, and closes the book.

Russell gets up, puts out a hand and ruffles her hair briefly. "You going to bed? Sleep well."

As he goes out, Molly says, "Russ—don't tell anyone. About the book."

He pauses, looking back at her with his quirky eyebrows raised. "Okay. Why?"

"I don't know. I'd just like it to be my private thing."

"You're a funny kid," Russell says indulgently. "Sure—I'm as silent as the grave." And she knows, as he leaves, that his mind has already run on to other far more immediate concerns than her broken book and its long-dead owner.

But for her, something magical has happened, something that links her back to her lost land, something that feels like the opening of a strange perilous door.

SAM

1803

ALL THAT FIRST NIGHT AND HALF THE NEXT DAY THEY KEPT
US PENNED DOWN THERE IN THE DEPTHS OF THE SHIP, WITH NO
more food but some more water, and two other buckets in
which to piss. I was sick as a dog still, from the stench and
from the swaying of the ship, and the men who had been
drunk when they were caught were groaning and even howl-
ing with pain and fury. It was a miserable, reeking bunch of
men who were herded up on deck by two marines sometime in
the next afternoon.

I shall never forget that day. The sky was grey, but dazzling
after the darkness below. Blinking, we came staggering out into

the world of the Royal Navy: a line of marines drawn up, all red and gleaming white; the mocking, watching faces of many seamen, and a table, an ordinary table, looking very strange there on the deck of a ship, with three officers sitting at it. The one in the middle looked so grand that I thought he must be the captain of HMS *Victory*. He had a straight nose and a strong mouth, long brown hair tied with a black ribbon, and a cockade in his hat, and his coat was blue with white lapels and gold anchor buttons. He was the finest man I had ever seen.

The seaman in charge of us pulled off his hat. "Twenty-seven pressed men, Your Honor," he said.

The officer looked at us, turning his head slowly to survey the whole group. "Gentlemen," he said clearly, "you are aboard His Majesty's Ship Victory, under the command of Captain Samuel Sutton, and I am First Lieutenant Quilliam." He paused, glancing at the officer beside him, and his voice changed. "Dear God, what a sorry bunch," he said. "Sort them, if you please, Mr. Smith."

Mr. Smith was a thin-faced man in a plain dark coat; later I found out that he was one of the ship's surgeons. He came round to the front of the table and began pointing at us.

"You, and you—step forward—and you—" He picked out seven of us, including my uncle and me, and the marines pushed us to stand in front of the others.

Mr. Smith said curtly, "Take the rest—strip and wash." And I saw now that farther along the deck, grinning sailors waited with buckets and brushes. A hubbub of orders and protest and laughter began, and without ceremony all the other captives were seized and stripped of their clothes, and scrubbed clean. They hopped around, naked, shivering. But certainly they had been a filthy lot, with dirt-encrusted clothes and greasy hair. I realized that those of us separated out by Mr. Smith the surgeon were the only decent-looking human beings in the group—and I felt an extra wave of gratitude toward my uncle, whose first act on taking me into his home had been to set me naked in a bath and have me wash my body and my hair clean with soap, in water that to my astonishment was warm. After that, he and my aunt had given me clean clothes, and thrown my old ones away.

My uncle was standing now in front of the first lieutenant, who was checking his name on a list.

"Well, Charles Davis," he said, "are you prepared to take the bounty and serve your country in His Majesty's Navy?"

My uncle took a deep breath, and touched his fingers to his forehead in a sort of salute. "Begging your pardon, sir, I have been serving my country making rope in His Majesty's Dockyard these past fifteen years—rope for this great ship you command, too."

The sailor in charge of us made a growling noise at his having the audacity to speak so, but Lieutenant Quilliam looked at my uncle with interest.

"Have you indeed," he said. "Well, now you may follow that useful trade here, Charles. We can well use another roper."

My uncle said desperately, "I know nothing of the sea, sir."

Lieutenant Quilliam said, "I do not choose to waste a skilled rope-maker as a pressed land man. For a start, I shall write you down Ordinary Seaman, with five pounds bounty and a fair wage and chance of promotion, and you will follow your calling. But you must enter the Service."

His eyes held my uncle's for a long moment, and as I looked at my uncle's face I saw him lose all hope of his secure ropewalk life and his wife and home, all in that instant. He even answered like a sailor. "Aye aye, sir," he said.

"Sign your name here."

So my uncle Charlie signed.

"Good man," said the first lieutenant, and motioned him farther down the table, to the men who would measure his height and chest and write down the color of his eyes and hair, all so that he could be listed and captured as a deserter if he ran away.

And there was I, standing in turn in front of the great man.

He looked at my name on his list. "Samuel Robbins," he said. "Are you for a life of adventure, boy? Will you take the King's shilling?"

"The other officer told me seven pounds a year, Your Honor," I said without thinking, and the sailor in charge instantly cuffed me round the head. But the lieutenant held up his hand to stop him, and looked me in the eye. I think he was trying not to smile.

"He was right," he said. "The shilling is a token. Seven pounds a year for a boy, if you join the Service."

I looked for my uncle, but I couldn't see him in the crowd of men. "I will do the same as my uncle, sir, if you please."

"The roper is your uncle? Are you apprenticed?"

"No, sir. I was just starting. He brought me from the country a week ago."

"I was a country boy myself once," Lieutenant Quilliam said. He handed me a pen. "Make your mark here."

"I can write, sir," I said, proud of myself that I could say so, and I wrote my name. The lieutenant gave me another close look and nodded me down the line.

And so I became a sailor.

HMS *Victory* was so huge, I felt like a lost ant in a giant ant-hill. On deck, all I could see or think about was the great singing mass of ropes and canvas overhead, the three towering, swaying masts, and the hundreds of men shinning up and down the rigging to release the sails or furl them. Below, the ship was a dark complicated world, down and down, one deck after another, all lined with black iron cannons and intent men bustling along on mysterious errands. It was three days before I saw my uncle again.

The first day was a blur of shouted orders and muddle, as two other new boys and I were sent from one place to another to be issued hammocks, shown how and where to stow them, taught the way to the part of the upper gundeck where we would sleep and eat. And because HMS *Victory* had sailed out of the Medway estuary now, all the time the floors were slanting and tossing, and I was trying not to slide or crash into a stairway, or be sick.

And very soon, work began. Because I was a country boy and ignorant of the sea, they gave me to the ship's cook, to help look after the chickens and do anything else he wanted. There was not only live poultry aboard the ship, but animals too, so that there would be eggs and fresh meat for the officers. (Fresh meat for the men too, when a voyage began, but soon they had only tough salt beef and pork that had been stored in casks, sometimes for years.) Somewhere on board there were ducks and geese, sheep and pigs, but Charles Carroll, the ship's cook, kept the best of the chickens two decks down to be handy to his galley, a stuffy little world framed by an enormous iron stove set on a tiled floor.

So there I was sent, with another boy called Stephen, a small, weaselly little fellow with darting black eyes that never looked at you straight on. Carroll the cook was an oldish man, completely bald, with a wooden leg and a rasping voice; he looked as though he would lay you flat with one of his broad hands if you so much as sneezed at the wrong moment. When we were delivered to him as helpers, he looked at us without enthusiasm, spat into the fire his assistant was lighting in the stove, and said curtly, "Can you kill and pluck a fowl?"

"Oh yes, sir!" piped Stephen, so quickly that I doubted this was true.

"Get on, then. Two of the hens, and look sharp about it. They're up the stairs there. And I want the feathers saved."

Stephen scuttled off. I paused. "Sir—we'll need knives, and a bucket—and hot water—"

Carroll reached out to an array of kitchen tools hanging on a rack, dropped a small axe and a knife into a wooden bucket, and thrust it at me. "Everything out of this galley comes straight back, or you get a thrashing," he said.

"Yes, sir."

"Draw them hot water, Tommy," he said to his assistant, and I looked at the man properly and could hardly move for surprise. All his skin was shiny black—his face, his neck, his hands, everything—and I had never seen such a thing before.

Tommy saw my ignorance at once, I think, and grinned at me: a broad white grin full of gleaming teeth. It made me grin back, before I ran up the stairs.

It was easy to find the chickens; they were cackling wildly in a row of wooden cages, as Stephen groped inside one of their doors. I could see he had the wrong cage; the hens were white, and all cozied up with straw to protect their eggs.

"Not those, they're the layers. Here—" I opened a cage with black and whites like those we used to kill on the farm for dinners at the great house. I grabbed one of the hens and brought it out, kicking; then I held it across to Stephen. "You want to wring its neck?"

He shook his head, staring. He was a real city boy, you could tell. He'd probably never even seen a live chicken before. I didn't blame him for not wanting to kill it; that was the one job on the farm that I had really hated. But I'd had to do it then, and I had to do it now.

My father had been able to grab a chicken's head in his big hand and swing its body round in a swift circle to break its neck in a flash, but my hands weren't strong enough to do that. Next to the cages there was a block of wood, stained dark; I knew what that must be for. "Hold tight," I said to Stephen, "very tight"—and I put the struggling hen into his hands, stretched its neck out over the block and brought down the axe as hard as I could, to kill it fast. To my relief the head fell away—and Stephen shrieked, for the headless bird in his hands was still kicking, with blood splashing out. They often do that, even after they're dead. Just as Stephen dropped it I shoved the bucket underneath, and as it went on twitching in there he turned his head away and retched. But he didn't throw up, though his face was pasty white.

"Good," I said, to encourage him. "Now one more."

And we did it again. As the second hen's body was bouncing around on top of the first, Tommy came up the stairway with a bucket of hot water in one hand and a mop in the other. He looked at the birds, nodded, and took the axe out of my hand.

"Clean up well when you done," he said. He had a funny accent, like singing. "All this ship have to be clean as a whistle, all the time, or we get the cat."

"The cat?" I said.

"Cat-o'-nine-tails," Tommy said, and made a horrible face. "Flogging, by a whip wi' nine lashes to it. Or for boys, a beating with cane."

He put the mop into Stephen's hands, and we both knew without speaking that we would make sure to use it well.

So then I got the birds into the bucket of water while it was still hot, and showed Stephen how to pluck the feathers. He was slow and clumsy but he tried hard, and I began to think he might be better than his sly looks. He was a city boy sure enough; he said he had been living on the streets for half a year after running away from home. He was thirteen years old but very small for his age. He had been caught stealing bread, and put into the Navy instead of prison or a poorhouse.

But we were all in prison on this ship, really.

When we delivered the two naked hens to the cook, with their giblets and feathers clean and separate, I suppose he thought we were worth having as help. He set me to feeding the chickens, cleaning out their cages and collecting the eggs—with promises of a beating if I ever broke or stole one—while Stephen scoured pots and scrubbed the tiled floor. Within a day we were mucking out the pigs and the sheep too, and we soon found we had one of the worst jobs on the ship.

I had to be out of my hammock before sunrise and get to the galley by four in the morning. That was when Mr. Carroll and Tommy began to light the fire and heat water for the men's breakfast. After that the whole day was full of messy, reeking work, through dinner at noon, supper at four o'clock and bedtime at eight. As boys we were classified as "idlers"—a poor joke, considering how hard we worked. Idlers are the lowest form of life in the Royal Navy: the people who do all the jobs that have nothing to do with sailing the ship. And as third-class boys—there were three classes—we were the lowest of the low.

About thirty of us boys slept on the upper gundeck, right underneath the ship's deck, in canvas hammocks slung above the shining black cannons that poked their muzzles out all along both sides of the ship. They were big guns, firing iron balls that weighed twelve pounds each—though the guns on the decks below were much bigger, twenty-four-pounders on the middle gundeck and huge thirty-two-pounders on the lower. When they had gunnery practice Stephen and I had to keep out of the way, but the noise was stupendous and I longed to watch those powerful cannons being fired. Nearly every other boy was attached to a gun crew as a "powder monkey," to fetch gunpowder every time the gun was fired. I was very envious of them.

The leader of the boys seemed to be a redhead called William Pope; he and a bunch of his friends bossed us all around. They stole anyone's jacket or shirt if they fancied it, or any little keepsake a boy had from home, like a knife or a kerchief, making me almost glad I had nothing but the clothes I stood up in—and slept in too, most nights. We had to wash our clothes and ourselves once a week for inspection, but otherwise there wasn't time. Stephen and I smelled bad as a result, so the bigger boys made life miserable for us. Even though some of them had disgusting jobs of their own, they would scream and honk and hold their noses when we came near.

"Shite smells bad enough," said William Pope, shoving me away from him as I passed, "but pig-shite is worse!"

So we had to sling our hammocks in a tiny cramped space next to the far bulkhead, just the two of us. Though maybe that was better than hanging close-packed like the others, so tight together that if you so much as coughed you would set the whole line of hammocks swinging.

I had never thought, at home, that I would ever miss our crowded straw mattress. I wondered often if my little sisters missed me, and whether they had to go to school now unprotected—or if they went at all. As for my mother, I ached with longing when I thought of her, and sometimes—quietly, in the dark—I wept.

It was a dark, stuffy, tilting world we boys lived in. Up on deck the business of the ship went on: every officer and man followed his exact ordered routine, and the real sailors, the topmen, the fo'c'slemen and the afterguard, clambered up and down the rigging of those towering masts amazingly fast, controlling the sails. The ship's whole true life was up there. But I was hardly ever free to go up to the fresh air; Mr. Carroll always had some nasty below-decks work for me to do.

I was the boy in Mr. Carroll's mess—the men all ate their

meals in groups of four or six, called messes, and many of them had a boy attached, to do the dirty work. We did jobs like cleaning out the spittoon, the bucket they spat tobacco-juice into. One of their two pleasures was chewing a chunk of solid tobacco, very slowly, spitting out the brown juice from time to time until the tobacco disintegrated and the bits had to be spat out too. The other pleasure was drinking rum, which was issued to every man jack of us twice a day—half a ration for boys—diluted with water and called grog. You could drink your grog there and then or keep it for a swap. Most of us boys swapped it, though we were also allowed to have money added to our pay instead of being issued grog.

Mr. Carroll was given so many tots of grog in exchange for little treats from the galley that he was nearly always half drunk. He was clever at keeping himself sober at inspection time, when any visibly drunk man would be ordered a dozen lashes, but Stephen and I knew all too well that he would be drunk half an hour afterward, raging at us and at Tommy. Once he broke a big wooden ladle over my back, and once he threw a pot of hot water at Stephen, scalding him so badly that he had to go to the surgeon for the hurt skin to be dressed. Stephen told the surgeon it was an accident. I had argued that he should say what really happened, and he said I was a fool; that the cook would deny it and call him a lying little rogue, which any officer would believe because there would be no proof against it, and then the cook would beat him half to death. He was probably right.

But worse than the cook was one of the midshipmen, Oliver Pickin. HMS *Victory* had about twenty midshipmen; they were in training to be officers someday, but they had to learn to do everything the sailors did, including climbing to the tops of the masts. Some of them were as young as Stephen and me, some were quite old, but most were young men, wild and rash and looking for anyone they could mistreat in the way that they were often mistreated themselves. Oliver Pickin reminded me of my brother Dick; he was about the same size and just as mean-spirited. The only time I felt sorry for redheaded William Pope was when young Mr. Pickin one day got William a dozen strokes of the cane for failing to salute him. Of course William hadn't saluted him; he'd been staggering along with an armful of hammocks that stopped him from seeing anything, let alone saluting it.

Within four weeks of our sailing from Chatham we were headed south through stormy weather into the Bay of Biscay. We had put in to Portsmouth and Vice-Admiral Lord Nelson had come aboard. I knew by now that Nelson was the hero of the Royal Navy, and of all England too, though back on the farm I had scarcely even known that we were at war with the French. He had won great victories at the Battle of the Nile and at Copenhagen, and lost his right arm and the sight of his right eye in battle, and all the men loved him. When they talked of "the Admiral" it was Nelson they meant, even though there were full admirals like Lord Collingwood who held higher rank.

At first, I saw no more of Lord Nelson than a small figure on the quarterdeck at inspection, with stars and decorations gleaming on his blue coat. That first day he came aboard, war was declared on France again after a few weeks of peace, and all the men cheered. Then we sailed across the English Channel to

meet Lord Collingwood's fleet, and the Admiral left us again
before we even found them. Word was that he was taking command of the fleet in the Mediterranean, and was in a hurry to get
down there and fight the French. So he went aboard Captain
Hardy's frigate *Amphion*, smaller and faster than big old
Victory, and they sailed south.

When Captain Sutton found Lord Collingwood, we were
sent south too. The wind was good but strong, and these were
stormy waters, so *Victory*'s decks were wildly atilt most of the
time, a hard matter for those of us set often to carrying things
(and harder still for the sailors sent up the rigging.) Lurching
over the deck one day with two buckets of swill for the pigs, I
was passing Oliver Pickin and an older midshipman, Mr.
Harrington, when a furious gust of wind sent Harrington and
me both tumbling on top of Pickin, with the pigswill from my
buckets splashing over all three of us.

Pickin cried out in fury, and scrambled up and began lash-
ing at me with his cane. Harrington protested: "Oliver, for
God's sake—the boy fell, and so did we—it's not his doing!"

Pickin was beside himself. "Clumsy little whoreson—"

"Stop!" yelled Harrington, and held his arm.

And Pickin did stop, but glared at me as I scurried away to
find a mop, and I knew he would not forget.

Nor did he. Two days later word came to the galley that the
captain's cook wanted a dozen eggs, and Mr. Carroll sent me up
with them. It was a long way, the captain's quarters being in the
stern of the ship and the galley way forward. I was making my
way cautiously along the deck, holding the wooden rack of
eggs with both my hands, when the whistles of the bosun's

mates shrilled for the men to reduce sail. I stood frozen beside one of the great deck-top carronades as dozens of seamen came running for the rigging, and seeing my plight they tried to steer clear of me. Most of them were good fellows when sober, and knew from their own experience what a whipping I would get if I broke even one of those eggs.

But when I dodged out again, a foot was stuck suddenly between my own, and tripped me, and the eggs and their frame went smashing down on the deck as I fell. I wailed in horror, and as I scrambled up, a hand took tight hold of my ear. "It's the clumsy pig boy!" cried Midshipman Oliver Pickin, grinning, and I knew beyond doubt that it was his foot that had brought me down.

I wrenched my head away. "You tripped me! You did that!"

"Are you accusing me, brat?"

"Those eggs were for the *captain*—"

Pickin looked round, his face full of triumph and malice. "Insolence to an officer!" he cried. He grabbed at a couple of sailors who were running for the mast. "Clap hold of him, you!"

A bosun's mate was in full cry after the sailors, flicking at them with his cane. "Up with you, you idle scum! Aloft there!" He paused as he saw Pickin.

"Insolence!" the midshipman was yelling. "Insolence! A bar in his mouth for three days! You—take this fellow's name!"

The bosun's mate looked at me and at Pickin, and I knew there was nothing he could do for me: Oliver Pickin was a bullying malicious midshipman but he was an officer, and the rules of the Royal Navy were rock hard.

And so it was that for two full days and nights I had to go

about the ship with a five-inch iron bolt forced across my open mouth and tied with yarn behind my head, like a bit in the mouth of a horse. I could neither eat nor drink, and at night I could not sleep for the pain. Stephen and two or three of the other boys were good to me, and gently spooned water into my mouth so that I should not totally parch, but I was wretched beyond belief. I felt there was no hope in life; that I was doomed to the Navy and its injustices forever. I thought seriously of throwing myself into the sea, where I should drown very fast because I could not swim.

I crawled into a corner of the gundeck alone, in despair, and I wept.

And there my uncle found me. In all the weeks since we were pressed, we had seen each other only for brief moments, through the demands of his work and my own, and though he knew of the bad state I was in, there was nothing he could do about it. This time, though, as he looked into my dirty distorted face, there was an angry set to his mouth that I had never seen before.

"I know what led to this, Sam," he said. "One of my mates was watching. I think I can do something. Have faith—by tomorrow there may be help."

With a damp rag he wiped my chin clear of the blood that kept trickling down from where the metal cut into my lips. Then looking angrier still, he hurried away.

At the end of the next day, when we were slinging our hammocks, with Stephen helping me because I was so weak at the knees after working without food, big William Pope came up behind me and put his hands on my shoulders. I stopped still, wary, and then I felt his fingers at the back of my head, untying the tight yarn. He turned me to face him, and eased the iron bolt carefully out of my mouth. One of my teeth came with it; knocked loose when the bolt was put in, it had been held in place only by the bolt itself.

Our Scottish boy Colin Turner was there too, watching wide-eyed, with two wooden mugs in his hands. William sat me down on a cask, took one of the mugs from Colin and held it to my mouth.

I said thickly, "What is it?"

"Drink," said William. "Go on. Little sips."

So I did. It was warm, and seemed to spread comfort through my whole body as it trickled down my throat.

"Portable soup," Colin said, "to make you better." And I remembered that he was boy to the surgeons' mates, and guessed that he had begged or stolen this from their store. Portable soup was a kind of dried jelly that became a thin beef broth when added to hot water; it was given to patients in the sick bay to strengthen them.

When I had drunk it all down, sitting there on the cask like a limp bundle of rags, I looked at the others and found tears coming out of my eyes, not of misery this time but of gratitude and relief. "Thank you," I said. "Oh thank you."

"Bosun's orders, the first I ever was glad to get," William said. "And they are changing your mess, putting you with the ropers and sailmakers. Stephen is to take your place eating with the cook."

Stephen made a wry face, but grinned at me. "It will be no worse than the pigs," he said.

William put the other mug into my hand. "Grog, to help

you sleep," he said. "Drink it down quick before someone catches us."

So I slept that night like a baby, perhaps for the first time since I had been one. And the next day, though I had thought it impossible, my life changed once more.

Molly

IN CONNECTICUT

MOLLY WAKES UP THE NEXT MORNING OUT OF A DREAM THAT SHE CANNOT REMEMBER, WITH A SOUND RINGING THROUGH HER head: the double stroke of a bell, repeated. *Bong-bong, bong-bong, bong-bong* . . . She feels she has heard it before, but she doesn't know where.

Sunshine is spilling around the edges of the blinds into the cheery yellow-white bedroom. It's early morning: six-thirty, her alarm clock tells her. She lies there on her back for a little while, looking at the picture on the wall at the foot of her bed: a framed photograph of her mother and father on a beach somewhere. They are laughing, and in her father's arms is a chubby smiling baby. The baby is Molly, though it looks rather like Donald.

Molly feels drained, empty, as if something had washed all feeling out of her. It is the way she felt yesterday after all that crying; it has survived her night's sleep. But jumping out of her memory comes the discovery of the little square of cloth inside her Nelson book, and the emptiness is suddenly filled. *Awesome!* says a voice inside her head, and she wants to jump up and tell the whole world. At the very least she wants to e-mail her friends Sally, Jen and Naomi, and send off a letter to her grand-parents, who prefer paper to computers.

But at the same time she feels strongly again that she should tell nobody at all; that it's a pity even Russell knows.

Why? she wonders.

Not yet! says the voice in her head, offering no reason.

She gets out of bed and goes to her desk. There is the book, with its damaged blue cover and the little brown envelope inside, hidden away in the dark for so long but now revealed. Today she will start reading about Nelson. Now that she has a piece of his ship's flag, she has a powerful urge to find out what he was like.

Molly goes downstairs in her pajamas to get some orange juice, and she is only halfway down the stairs when she realizes that the one person she must tell about her discovery is Mr. Waterford.

Kate is in the kitchen, feeding Donald small spoonfuls of cereal. He gurgles at Molly, and bangs the table of his high chair. Kate puts out an arm and gives Molly a hug. "I forgot to remind you, you're babysitting," she says. "I'm taking Russ to his driving test."

"No problem," says Molly, and she thinks: *Russell! He'll have his license, he can drive me to see Mr. Waterford!*

Kate still has her arm around her. "You're such a good girl," she says, and squeezes her again. Then she lets her go, and Molly heads for the refrigerator.

"We'll leave about eight-fifteen," Kate says. "Back by eleven. I've changed Donald. Put him down for a nap when he starts to fuss."

"Okay," says Molly. She pours herself some juice, kisses Donald on the nose and sits at the kitchen table. Kate says hesitantly, "Are you all right, love?"

Molly looks up. There is an odd expression on her mother's face, as if she were far more concerned about Molly than a small babysitting job deserves. And so she is. Kate was deeply troubled by yesterday's outburst of grief; it was far more serious than anything she has ever seen happen to a child. She has been awake half the night worrying about it.

Molly says, "I'm fine."

"I had a long talk with Carl this morning," Kate says. She sits down.

"In Italy?"

"It's lunchtime there. We decided . . . Darling, how would you like it if you and Donald and I made a quick trip to see Granny and Grandad before you start school?"

Molly stares at her. A miracle has exploded into her life like a meteor. She can hardly believe it. "To London? Really?"

"Really," Kate says, and finds her daughter's arms wound around her neck, so tightly that she splutters. Donald wails. Molly gives him another kiss.

"We're going home!" she tells him. "We're going home!"

"Just for a week," Kate says cautiously.

Molly says, "That's *wonderful!*"

Donald is fast asleep in his crib, sucking his thumb, and Molly is downstairs again, listening as the sucking sounds grow gradually fainter over the baby monitor. When the outside door bursts open, she can tell instantly from the look on Russell's face that he has failed his driving test. He heads for the refrigerator, scowling, and pulls out the carton of orange juice.

"Poor Russ," Kate says, coming in after him. "He drove very well but he got a very picky examiner."

"He's a jerk!" Russell says, pouring juice so crossly that it splashes over the edge of the glass. "A pompous jerk!"

Molly says, "What happened?"

Russell gives an explosive angry grunt and drinks his juice. Kate says, "Russ had to turn left, and he was really careful to make a hand signal, because the examiner had reminded him to be sure to do that. But he didn't put on his flasher as well, so the man failed him."

"He said that stuff about hand signals just to throw me," Russell says bitterly. "And he kept calling me Carl."

"Well, it *is* your first name," Kate says mildly. "He wasn't to know we don't use it."

"Stop by that lamppost, Carl! Carl, we're going to turn left at the light!" Russell makes his angry grunt again. Looking at him, Molly sees an echo of her stepfather in the straight nose and lean jawline, and the shape of those arched eyebrows.

At the same time it occurs to her that Russ will not now be

able to drive her to see Mr. Waterford, and that she cannot possibly ask Carl or her mother to take her there.

Later that day, Molly begins to read *The Life of Nelson*. She discovers that Horatio Nelson was born in Norfolk, and that when he was a small boy and was punished for stealing pears from his schoolmaster's pear-tree, he said he "only took them because every other boy was afraid."

Then she turns the page and comes across the bookmark that Mr. Waterford put inside the book when he sold it to her. She remembers the way he smiled at her as he did so. The bookmark is tucked so securely between two pages that it has even survived the book's disastrous crash when she threw it at Jack. Molly looks at the bookmark, and sees printed on it the name and address of Mr. Waterford's shop, his telephone and fax numbers—and his e-mail address.

So she turns on her computer and writes him an e-mail.

Dear Mr. Waterford, she writes, *I am Molly Jennings, the English girl who bought Robert Southey's The Life of Nelson. Something amazing has happened. Hidden inside the front of the book there was a sort of envelope with a piece of cloth inside that is a piece of HMS Victory's flag at Trafalgar. . . .*

. . . and she tells him about the inscription, and Emma's note about her father Samuel Robbins—and then, taking a deep breath, she types out the question that is her real reason for wanting to talk to him.

Is it still all right for me to keep this book? she writes.

She is so nervous about the answer she may get to this question that she hits the "Send" button even before she has signed the e-mail. And off it goes, irrevocably launched into the ether, on that mysterious instant journey taken by all e-mails.

There is a tap at the door, and Kate puts her head in. "Want to come and get a pizza, darling? Russ has a sailboat race at two, so I thought we'd all have lunch on the way."

"Sure," Molly says. She puts the computer to sleep. It's too much to hope that Mr. Waterford will send her an instant reply.

"Russ can drive us," Kate says. "I told him it's like getting back on the horse after you've fallen off."

Molly and Kate sit on the balcony of the yacht club, watching the small white sails tack to and fro out in the bay. They have no idea which boat is Russell's, or who is winning, but they feel family loyalty demands that they watch the races.

"We're showing the flag for Russell," Kate says, rocking Donald gently in his stroller. She smiles. "What a lot of phrases we use that come from the Navy. Keeping an even keel. Putting your oar in."

"All in the same boat," says Molly, inspired. "Clearing the decks."

There is a faint muffled bang out on the water, and they both peer, but can see nothing to tell them whether this is signaling the beginning or end of a race.

"Mum," Molly says, "when are we going to London?"

"The travel agent's working on it. If she can find tickets that don't cost a fortune we'll go next week, I guess." Kate looks at the happiness in her daughter's face, and smiles ruefully. "Oh darling," she says, "I do hope you won't feel horribly let down when we come back again."

"No!" Molly says. Coming back is an image that has not yet been given any place in her mind; she is too busy thinking of arriving.

"Hi, Kate!" says a hearty male voice, and they look up to see a tall, balding man in khaki shorts and a green short-sleeved shirt. He is beaming at them. Beside him is a lean, deeply tanned lady wearing several necklaces and bracelets.

"Hi!" says Kate brightly, and Molly knows instantly that her mother has no idea who these people are.

"Russell steered to victory!" says the necklaced lady in a voice almost as deep as her husband's. She smiles. She has amazingly white teeth.

"He did? I couldn't tell. That's great!" Kate clutches Molly as if she were a lifebelt. She says, "Have you met my daughter Molly?"

Molly is familiar with this gambit for discovering names, and is relieved to find that it works. The man thrusts out his hand to her and says amiably, "Hi, Molly. I'm Bradenham Parker, old friend of Carl's. This is m'wife Muffie."

Molly shakes his hand. Muffie Parker gives her a brief smile and nod, and leans past her to chuck Donald under the chin. "And this is your little son!" she says to Kate. "Russell's future crew!"

"Yes, I dare say," Kate says.

Molly says in a clear voice, "His name is Donald."

Mrs. Parker jingles a bracelet at Donald. "Hello, Donnie sweetie!"

Donald looks obligingly angelic, and blows a bubble.

Mr. Parker says heartily, "How are you settling in, Molly? Having a busy summer?"

"We're going to London next week!" says Molly happily.

"Already?" says jingling Mrs. Parker. "You only just got here!" Her dark eyes survey both Molly and Kate critically, inquisitively.

"Lighten up, Muffie!" says Mr. Parker. "Two weeks into our honeymoon you ran back to Boston, remember? Said you missed the cat." He gives a sudden bray of laughter.

"Get lost, Brad," says Mrs. Parker. She burrows into a very large canvas bag hanging from her shoulder, and produces a pair of binoculars, through which she proceeds to stare at the water. "There they are," she says. "Russ has let Jack take the helm. Big mistake."

Mr. Parker opens his mouth and shuts it again, looking reproachful, and Molly realizes that these are the parents of the abominable Jack. No wonder he is the way he is. She crouches beside Donald, pretending to amuse him, hoping they will go away. Very soon they do.

Kate sighs. "That lady is going to spread rumors that poor dear Carl Hibbert's new wife and daughter are already leaving him. After six weeks, my dear!"

"Nobody will believe her," Molly says indignantly. She pauses. "Will they?"

"Nobody who matters," Kate says. "I'm going to change Donald—back in a minute."

So she disappears with the stroller, and Molly looks out at the white dots on the grey water and thinks about England. She feels guilty that her mother is making this transatlantic trip solely on her behalf, but not guilty enough to give it up. The prospect of being in London again has filled her world with hope.

She looks out to sea, beyond the boats. Strictly speaking this is not the sea but Long Island Sound, she knows; Long Island lies somewhere out there, between here and the Atlantic Ocean. But a haze of heat has blurred water and air so that the horizon is lost in a band of grey-white mist, and suddenly from that mist Molly hears a distant boom, like the sound of a massive gun.

She squints into the distance. For a moment she sees through the haze the outline of a great sailing ship, three-masted, square-rigged, with a dim cloud of smoke drifting away from its side. Molly catches her breath; she has never seen anything like it except in pictures.

Then it is gone. Molly strains to see more, but there is only the water and the sky. She feels again an odd sense of being beckoned, as if some soundless voice were calling her. Where has the ship gone?

When they are driving home with a cheerful victorious Russell, she says to him, "Did you see that tall ship, way out?"

"What ship?" Russell says.

"It was on the horizon. Just like the picture in your room, the Tall Ships Race."

"That was six years ago—none of those ships is around now. *What* did you see?"

Molly looks away, out of the car window. "I expect I was imagining it," she says.

Back at the house, Molly goes to her computer and finds an e-mail from Mr. Waterford.

Of course you must keep the book, he writes. *You bought it, so you bought anything that came with it. I should tell you that a piece*

*of the Victory's flag was sold two years ago at Bonham's auction
house in London for a very large sum. Maybe yours will send you to
college. Take great care of it. Best wishes, Alan Waterford.*

Afterward there is a P.S.

*HMS Victory is still with us, you know. Perhaps you've been
there. They keep her in Portsmouth Harbour, wonderfully restored.*

Molly stares at this, and a vigorous ambition begins to form
in her mind. Then she sees that Mr. Waterford has added a second P.S. after the first.

I must confess, he writes, *that I should love to take a look at
your treasure, if you should ever be passing through Mystic again.*

So Molly writes back with a promise that she will visit
Mystic Seaport someday soon.

She sits there for a moment, thinking about the mysterious
sailing ship that showed itself to her so briefly, before disap-
pearing into the mist. Did HMS *Victory* look like that? But
HMS *Victory* is in Portsmouth. . . .

Very carefully, she takes the little ragged piece of cloth out
of its antique homemade envelope inside her *Life of Nelson.* It
gives her a very strange sensation, as if it connects her in some
way to all the events it has seen and survived. And perhaps to
more than that. Lying there on her desk, it is a very ordinary
scrap of dirty-looking material that any unknowing person
would toss into the garbage, and yet Molly feels that it is almost
a living thing. She has a strong urge to take it with her to
Britain.

But when the time comes to pack for their flight, a week later,
Molly finds herself overcome by anxiety that something would

happen to the piece of flag if she were to take it with her. Her mind keeps throwing up objections, even after she has finished packing and changed into her pajamas. If it were in her suitcase, the suitcase might go astray. If instead she put it in her carry-on bag, some security person might search the bag and accidentally damage the little piece of cloth—or, worse, take it, or throw it away. If she carried it in her pocket, she might crush it, or lose it, or her pocket might be picked. . . .

The book lies on her bed next to the suitcase. Molly stares at it, her mind veering round in circles like a confused compass needle.

Kate taps at the door and sticks her head in. "Are you packed? Get some sleep—we have to be up at five."

"Mmf," Molly says. "I'm nearly finished."

"Bed," says Kate, and goes away again.

So Molly, forced to instant decision, inspects her wounded book to make sure the envelope is safely tucked inside its cover, and slips it carefully onto a shelf of her favorite books, between *Bridge to Terabithia* and *Tehanu,* volumes she feels a wandering Russell or Carl would be unlikely to disturb. Now it will be safe until her return, unless the house burns down, which is one possibility she refuses to take seriously. She feels relieved that she will no longer have to watch and worry about her treasure, and she scrambles into bed in a glow of happy imaginings about the next day.

Just before she falls asleep she realizes that she must be feeling exactly as the grownup Sam Robbins had felt, leaving his precious bit of Nelson in his daughter's safekeeping before he sailed away once more. It is a sharing—and a powerful connection, for if Sam had taken the flag with him on that last voyage, it would never have come into Molly's life at all.

As this thought flickers in and out of her dozing mind, a sense of longing floods after it, full of pain, like a voice calling. But Molly does not hear, because she is asleep.

Kate has given Molly the seat beside the window. As the big plane tilts down through a grey mist of cloud, suddenly below her Molly sees the green patchwork of fields that is unmistakably England. *I'm home!* she thinks. *Home!* And all through the long slow descent she looks for London, finding it at last only in the proliferation of the rows of houses, with the red tiled roofs that she does not see in America, and the looping curves of the River Thames. She looks out at her country with love, and Kate, busy feeding Donald a bottle of watered juice to keep his ears from popping, glances at her face and feels a rush of pleasure mixed with guilt. Molly catches her eye, and gives her a brilliant smile.

At Heathrow Airport, Molly pushes Donald's stroller briskly along the pathway labeled FAST TRACK, reserved for holders of the red passports of the European Union. She is smugly aware that most of their fellow-travelers, American tourists, are penned behind a barrier in a waiting throng. Kate spreads their passports before the immigration officer at his desk, and he glances from Molly's passport picture to her glowing face. His eyes crinkle at the corners.

"Welcome home, Molly," he says.

And out beyond the baggage claim area, from which Molly pushes the stroller and Kate a baggage cart which would prefer to go sideways, there in the crowd is a bobbing trio of large white balloons. Each one is decorated with a firm black letter, *M* and *K* and *D*, and beneath them is the neat figure and smiling bearded face of Molly's grandfather.

After the first close joyous embraces, and that astonishing moment of rediscovering all the beloved lost details of a familiar face, Molly feels that she has never been away from her grandparents at all. The drive from the airport to their house in Highgate, in the north of London, is filled with excited chatter, and without question or pause for thought she carries her suitcase up the stairs to the little bedroom which has been "her" room, on visits to her grandparents' house, for as long as she can remember. Everything is the same. There at the dormer window is the ruffled white curtain, and the purple cushion on the window-seat; there across the room is the wardrobe where her spare jeans still hang, and her old sneakers wait. There is the bookshelf with her particular books that she always left at Granny and Grandad's house, and the cupboard with the outgrown still-loved toys. She looks at the battered lamb and giraffe and teddy-bear, and realizes with pleasure that soon Donald will be able to batter them some more.

She lies on her back on the bed, looking up at the constellations of stars that Grandad stuck on the ceiling for her when she was very small—and because she has been awake since five o'clock in the morning by American time, she falls asleep. Nobody wakes her up. They slip off her shoes and pull a quilt over her, and leave her there, sleeping in England.

"He's so different!" Granny says in wonder the next morning, with Donald in her arms. "In three months he's turned into a little person. Where did that little dribbling baby go?"

"He still dribbles," Kate says. "Buckets. I think he's cutting a tooth."

"That's what I mean!" says her mother. "Teeth! Next thing you know, he'll be playing football for Chelsea!"

Molly says with sudden bitterness, "We live in America. They'll teach him baseball."

"Now, now," says Kate. "They have football like ours—they just call it soccer."

"Grub up!" says Grandad, advancing on them with plates of bacon and eggs. "The full breakfast for your first morning, ladies." Long ago he and Granny had the wall between the kitchen and dining-room knocked down, and he has been busy at the kitchen end. In Molly's memories, he is always the cook. Her grandparents enjoy reversed roles, and it is her lean, athletic Granny who is likely to be found changing a fuse or washing the car, while Grandad is baking bread. His mince pies at Christmastime are legendary.

After breakfast, while Kate and her mother are upstairs giving Donald a bath, Grandad settles himself in his armchair with a cup of coffee—he makes excellent coffee too—and Molly sits companionably nearby, on the floor. Grandad looks down at her over his coffee-cup. He has deepset blue eyes below bristling grey eyebrows, and his neat beard is greyish-white with a darker line in the center. Molly thinks, *I never noticed that before.*

Grandad says, "Well, you have a week in England, my love—what shall we do with it? Where would you most like to go?"

Molly thinks about Lord Nelson and HMS *Victory*, but she has another image haunting her even more strongly. She says, "Can we go to the Round Pond?"

"Hampstead Heath is closer," Grandad says mildly.

Molly cocks her head and looks up at him. "You did ask," she points out.

"The Round Pond it shall be, this very day," Grandad says. "I just don't want you to be downcast, seeing Kensington."

The Round Pond, which is just what it sounds like, is in Kensington Gardens in central London, very close to the apartment in which Kate and Molly used to live. All through Molly's early childhood Kate would take her to play in Kensington Gardens, and almost until the day they left Britain they had gone for walks there, always taking bits of bread for any passing squirrel or duck.

She says, "Well, I might be downcast seeing Merton Square, but I don't want to go there. Just to the Gardens. Can I ring Jen, please? Maybe she can come too."

"Ring anyone you like," he says, "but give me a hug first." So Molly does, and leaves him to his coffee, and the ache of wishing that he could do something, anything, to cushion life for his uprooted granddaughter.

Before she left Connecticut, Molly e-mailed her three friends about her sudden trip to Britain, but she has heard from none of them, so now she telephones each one in turn, with her fingers crossed. But this is August, high holiday season in Britain, when half the inland population leaves home in search of sun and sea. She calls Jen's number, but the line is busy. At the next house she hears only Naomi's father's voice on the answering machine, with a pang of recognition. At Sally's house there is no answer at all, and when she calls Jen again she finds out why.

"Molly, dear!" cries Jen's mother, distant in Fulham. "How lovely to hear you! Jen will be so upset—she's in Spain with Sally's family, at that house they have. How long will you be home?"

Not long enough, Molly discovers, to see her best friend, who will not be back in the country until ten days from now. She thinks, as she hangs up the phone, *Jen liked me a lot better than she liked Sally, she'd never have gone if I were still here, not even for a house in Spain. . . .*

But that was then; this is now.

They put Donald in his stroller and they all go to Kensington Gardens, taking the Underground to Queensway, changing at Holborn. London is a very large city and this is a long trek; there were good reasons why Molly, living in Kensington, so often spent the night when visiting her grandparents in Highgate. But Molly is delighted to be back in a roaring, rocking underground train, rushing through the network of tunnels deep under the city, that is so familiar a part of life for Londoners that they call it simply The Tube. Donald is alarmed by the noise, and cries as the automatic doors slide shut, so Molly crouches beside his stroller in the swaying train and pulls funny faces, and plays "Where's Donald? . . . *There* he is!" until she makes him laugh. All the surrounding grownups watch, with nostalgia soft in their faces, except one thin man in a tight dark suit, who retreats behind a newspaper with a disdainful sniff.

And the sun is shining on Kensington Gardens, which is by

no means always the case, and Molly is happier than she has been for a long time as they turn from the busy streets, through the great wrought-iron gates, into the Broad Walk, with green grass and full-leafed trees stretching away on either side. Familiarity engulfs her, as if she were a stranded fish returned to the water. Although this is a weekday, the grass is littered with people: couples, families, solitary men or women—the men generally lying with their shirts stripped off, soaking up the sunshine—and everywhere children playing. Rollerbladers and skateboarders whizz along where they are allowed, on the Walk, and on the grass small boys and girls throw Frisbees or balls or chase one another about, shrieking. In one area Molly can see what looks suspiciously like a game of baseball. She does not investigate. With calm authority she leads her family toward the Round Pond, where she can see the white sails of large model yachts sailing serenely to and fro.

It is just as she remembered it. The bigger boats are operated mostly by elderly gentlemen, wearing jackets; one man even wears a suit and tie, as if he were on his way to work at a bank. They stand godlike with their remote controls, and their graceful vessels obediently tack about the Pond, without colliding. Only one of the yachts, slightly smaller than the rest, has a younger master; he is a boy of about sixteen, standing amongst a gaggle of admiring children, and he sends his boat on longer, faster swoops out of the way of the rest. Its sails are not white, but dark brown; it looks like a hawk among swans. Molly watches enviously. Something about the sixteen-year-old seems vaguely familiar; she thinks that perhaps he reminds her of Jack, and turns away.

"Molly! Over here!" It is her grandmother's clear positive voice, and Molly sees that her family has encamped itself beneath a tree—a young, modest tree still tethered to a post, with a hundred years or so to go before it matches the giant old trees elsewhere in the Gardens. Kate is spreading a dark green tartan blanket familiar to Molly from years of picnics, Grandad is unfolding two collapsible chairs, and Granny has begun ceremoniously opening the cooler and the old-fashioned wicker hamper that she took great pleasure in packing before they left. Donald is soon sprawled happily on the blanket, hauling himself onto all fours, rocking back and forth in a vain attempt to crawl. He looks like a trapped turtle. Molly beams at him. She feels an enormous sense of well-being.

They eat the feast that Granny has now unpacked: ham and tomato sandwiches, crunchy green beans, cheddar and (added by Grandad) Stilton cheese, apples, brown bread and chocolate, with blackcurrant soda for Molly and a thermos of tea for the rest. Grandad, a man of definite tastes, lingers over his chocolate, and an envious wasp zooms round his head trying to settle in his beard. Molly scrambles up from the blanket to escape the wasp, and finds herself colliding with an unexpected person approaching over the grass.

"Sorry!" he says. It is the boy from the Round Pond, holding his hawklike brown-sailed yacht by its mast; he lets it down to the ground, so that its hull leans against his leg. He gives Molly a brief grin of apology, but he is looking past her, at Kate. He says, "Er—Mrs. Jennings?"

Kate looks up, startled. She has been Mrs. Hibbert for two years now, and has begun to get used to it.

The boy says, "I'm Alex. Alex Stewart. We used to live in the ground-floor flat in Merton Square, do you remember? You knew my mum, her name is Mary. We have a golden retriever."

"Buster," Molly says, out of some deep well of memory. Now she realizes why this boy looked familiar.

He turns to her, surprised. He is almost grownup, with a faint dark shadow on his upper lip. "Excellent!" he says. "That's right. Buster's still around—he's pretty old, though. Fat and lazy. And you're Molly? You grew up."

"So did you," Molly says.

Kate says, "And you moved, didn't you?" She surfaces out of remembering. "Oh, I'm sorry—Alex, these are my parents, Mr. and Mrs. Blake."

Granny and Grandad and Alex Stewart all nod and smile at one another. "We bought a house in Fulham," Alex says. "But I sail the boat here, when I can."

"She's a beauty," Grandad says.

"Isn't she? I just got her, she's my biggest yet." He touches the brown mainsail with pride, and looks again at Kate. He says hesitantly, "That's why I had to come over when I saw you. It was your husband who got me started on boats, do you remember?"

Kate looks blank. "Did he?"

"Right here. He had a wonderful yacht. I was about eight, I think. He showed me the controls, he let me sail her all the way across the pond, I've never forgotten it. He got me hooked. My mum and dad had to buy me a boat the next Christmas. You were here, that first day, we all were, both families. Molly was very little, a toddler. We'd all come for a picnic, like you are now."

Granny holds out a plate. "Have a sandwich, Alex."

The boy laughs. "No, thank you, I must go. I just wanted to say hello." He picks up the boat again with his left hand, and holds out the right one to Kate, who shakes it. He adds, rather quick and low, "I was really sorry about Mr. Jennings."

"Thank you, Alex," Kate says.

To Molly's surprise, Alex Stewart puts out his hand to her too, and she takes it. The hand is big and hard, like Russell's. "Good-bye, Molly," he says. "Nice to see you."

"Good-bye."

They all watch him walk away, carrying the brown-sailed yacht that is almost as tall as Molly. "That was pleasant," Granny says.

Grandad nods. "Nice boy," he says.

"I didn't see any point in explaining about Carl, and America," Kate says.

"No, of course not."

Molly is not listening to them. She is gazing out at the Round Pond, seeing in her mind flickers of images that she had not known were there. A tall man with something in his hand, and a smaller figure beside him. A boat on the water, moving, its sail curving out white and full. She is very small, she is running toward the man, calling. But he does not look at her, not at this moment; he is looking out across the water, squinting into the sunlight, watching his boat dip and sway in the small waves.

And then he is gone.

SAM

1803–1805

F OR THE FIRST FEW WEEKS ON THE *VICTORY*, I HAD HATED THE SEA. I WAS NO LONGER SICK ALL THE TIME, BUT THE WEATHER continued foul as we sailed south. Day after day, the sea was so rough that the ship was always heeled over in one direction or the other, tipping so steeply that you could never walk without clutching at a bulkhead or a cannon. In some places there was netting to hang on to. The men would reach over their heads and grab a beam in the ceiling, but I was not quite tall enough. Sometimes I had to go on all fours. It was miserable all the way along the coast of France, and then of Spain and Portugal—not that I could see the coast, nor anything but waves and spray.

But gradually I got used to it and managed to stay upright. One day I saw Tommy laughing at me, as I skidded along the deck on my way to feed the chickens.

"You got your sea-legs, Sam!" he said, and I realized I had come half the length of the tilting ship without holding on to anything at all. Later that day, as we thrummed along under our creaking load of canvas, the clouds broke, and I saw the moon rise in the twilight sky. A big fat white moon it was, over the restless sea, and I looked at it through the dark mesh of rigging and thought that it was beautiful.

Then a bosun's mate flicked his cane against my bare legs and snarled, "Move, boy!" and I was back in the Navy again.

Though I still worked for the cook, I was no longer the slave of the mess at which he and his hangers-on ate. Thanks to my uncle and James Hartnell the rope-maker, I had a new family: the six men of their mess, number seventy-eight. I could hardly believe my good fortune. At the start of each month any man could change his mess, if he disliked the men he was with, or wanted to be with a friend elsewhere, but boys were not important enough to get that chance. I was just lucky that Lieutenant Quilliam had noted my connection to my uncle at the beginning—and it helped that we had joined the service, and were not written down as pressed men.

So now, at midday dinnertime and at supper, I would run down from the galley to the lower gundeck, where there was a roar of voices as the wooden mess tables were unhooked to swing down from the ceiling between the great cannons. The grog issue came right after dinner and supper, so these were the most cheerful times of the day. The men sat at benches on either side of the table; I sat on a barrel, at the end. They took turns weekly to be mess cook, the one responsible for bringing the food from the galley, and I used to go with each one of them; I was still a cook's boy, after all, and that was useful even if Mr. Carroll was in a bad mood. I helped to clean up too; the mess tables had to be spotless for inspection.

They were good men in that mess, none of them very young, all of them craftsmen. My uncle and Mr. Hartnell were the only rope-makers; the others were sailmakers. William Smith, a sturdy, amiable man from the West of England, was the master sailmaker; his mate was Andrew Scott, and Jonathan Stead was one of their crew—he was the oldest, a tall, stooped man with a thin fringe of hair round his bald head and a sad, lined face. In all the time I knew Jonathan I never saw him smile, not even at the funniest joke, not even after the second grog issue of the day. But he never cuffed me or even yelled at me, and when he found I had no knife of my own to eat with, he gave me an old one he had in his kit, after sharpening it very fine and giving it a canvas sheath so it would not cut me.

Early in the morning before breakfast, the mess cook went to collect sugar, butter, bread and flour for his mess from the purser's stores. If it was one of the four days of the week when we had meat, he also needed to pick out our share from the "steep tub" where chunks of salt pork or beef had been soaking overnight. To make this fair, every mess cook reached a long fork over the edge of the tub without looking, and he had to take the chunk that the fork pricked. A metal tag called a tally, with the number of his mess on it, was attached firmly to that chunk of meat, and along with all the rest it was boiled, for hours. Then at dinnertime we went to fetch it, and sometimes a bag of vegetables—also tagged—which had been boiling too.

Ship's bread, which was really a baked round biscuit as hard as wood, was kept near each mess table in a box called a "barge." Each mess had a keg of vinegar too, which was issued every two weeks. The water we drank was kept in casks in the hold and tasted worse and worse as it got older and older; it was a little bit better if you added some vinegar. And vinegar was useful for covering up the taste of the nastier kinds of food, too—like the brined cabbage, called "sour krout," that smelled so bad when a cask of it was first opened that men ran away if they saw one rolled out onto the deck. Mr. Smith made me eat the cabbage, though; he said it was an Admiral Nelson rule, to prevent scurvy, the disease which killed many seamen on long voyages.

I was used to horrible smells, from working in the galley—not to mention the pigsty. The first reek of the day came from the thin sticky gruel called "burgoo," that Mr. Carroll made every morning by boiling nasty oatmeal in stale water. It was a regulation breakfast, but the men in our mess hated it so much that they wouldn't eat it. Like a lot of other messes, they bribed the cook instead to blacken ship's bread over the galley fire, then grind it to a powder and boil it in water. We called this dark goop "Scotch coffee" and drank it with a little sugar, if we had any—and that, with a piece of the hard bread, was breakfast.

It could have been worse. On the farm we had often had no breakfast at all.

All morning, for the four meat days of the week, the galley stank of boiling salt pork or beef. When they first came out of their barrels, those fatty, gristly, bony chunks of meat were white with grains of salt, and as hard as rock, and even their overnight soaking didn't change them much. As they boiled away in the big coppers over the galley fire, the fat would rise to the top in an evil yellowish layer that Tommy had to skim off. Mr. Carroll didn't trust us boys to do it, because the fat, called "slush," was very valuable to him. Half of it was used to grease the ship's rigging, but the other half belonged by tradition to the ship's cook. He wasn't supposed to sell it to the men, but a lot of them were greedy for it, so of course he did. They spread it on their bread, or mixed it with flour to make a boiled pudding. Mr. Smith always made sure to buy some for our mess, but I wouldn't touch it; I'd spent too many hours scrubbing the coppers after Tommy had scraped out the last yellow layer of the awful stuff.

Almost every minute of every day on board ship was regulated, from the wake-up shake before dawn that sent Stephen and me to the galley, to supper before dusk and lights out four hours later. I was beginning to learn the strokes of the ship's bell, struck every half hour, that divided a day and night into six four-hour watches, but I still got muddled sometimes. The rhythm of each day was so much more exact than on the farm.

At weekends, everything was focused on Sunday morning inspection, before the church service. Every morning of the week we had to parade on deck in divisions, but on Sunday the inspection was truly fierce. You had to be shining clean and in a fresh shirt and trousers (and freshly shaved, though I didn't have to worry about that) or your name would be taken for punishment. So on Saturdays, we were given an hour after dinner to wash and mend our clothes, and the sailors with long hair plaited each other's pigtails smooth and neat. I was planning on a pigtail, but all I could do so far was tie my hair back in a little stub.

One Saturday I was mending a hole in my uncle's clean shirt, while he scrubbed his chest at a barrel of seawater shared with a group of others, and William Smith the sailmaker stopped to watch me.

"Ho," he said in his round Devon accent. "Look at thee, now. Middling good, for a rope-maker's boy."

"My mam used to make me help her with sewing," I said, flushing. "My sisters were too little." But then I realized with surprise that the expression on his face was not amusement, but interest.

"And hast a strong wrist? Push at my hand." He held out his big hand with the fingers pointing upward, palm toward me, and I held mine the same way and shoved my palm at his. I didn't last long, of course; he was strong as an ox.

My uncle shook his wet head, splashing us, and began rubbing himself dry with his dirty shirt. "Arm-wrestling with a boy, William?" he said.

"Charlie," said Mr. Smith, "I have a mind to steal this lad for a sailmaker."

"The service owns him, not me," said my uncle Charlie cheerfully. "We are not allowed him for roping—he has a talent for chickens." He grinned at me. He was not totally cast down by life in the Navy, even though he sorely missed my aunt; I think he was relieved to be still doing the work in which he took such pride. And the other men liked him.

William Smith snorted. "Chickens! When we go into battle the chickens go overboard—and the sails need mending."

"Overboard?" I said. "Is that true?" I was getting quite fond of my chickens—at least of the egg-layers, which I rarely had to kill.

"All the livestock," said Mr. Smith. He gave me a horrid leer, rolling his eyes, but I could see he was telling the truth. "Clear the decks for action, the order goes. Pigs and cannon don't mix."

"Oh." I felt sad for a moment. I had heard plenty of bloody stories about battles, from sailors who loved to try and terrify the boys, but nobody had mentioned chickens and pigs.

"So tha'll need a second occupation," said William Smith.

And that was how I came out of the bowels of the ship into the fresh air, far more often than before—for sailmaking needs space, and the sailmakers worked on deck whenever possible. William Smith had only to mention to the bosun, who had charge of all rigging and sails, that I might be useful to him, and half my galley duties vanished away. Every ship depended for its life upon its carpenters and sailmakers, and the masters of those crafts were warrant officers, who would stay with the ship even in peacetime, when the captain and officers would be let go. William Smith got what he wanted.

The cook grumbled loudly at losing half my time, but they gave him another of the boys, Hugh Portfield from Ireland, who had been cleaning the officers' cabins, and was glad of the change. And Stephen enjoyed ordering Hugh around. I still slept with the other boys, and big William Pope and I had become almost friends. I was closest to Stephen though. His street tricks were serving him well; he was quick and crafty, good at wheedling favors out of seamen in illegal exchange for his ration of grog—which by the strange laws of the Navy he was supposed to drink himself, even though he was so small that it would make him drunk, and drunkenness was a flogging offense. He was also, I noticed, beginning to pocket an occasional treat from the supplies that passed through the galley from the purser: an egg, or a chunk of the soft bread baked for the officers, or a piece of fruit.

"Be careful," I would say, and Stephen would laugh.

"Care killed the cat, Sam."

"I thought it was curiosity killed the cat."

"Well, it wasn't pinching an apple."

We were growing up fast, we boys, in some ways. We were certainly seeing the world, as Lieutenant Quilliam had promised me. Before long we had not only passed the whole of France, Portugal, and Spain, we had reached the Strait of Gibraltar, and were sailing in past the big rocky fortress that guards the entrance to the Mediterranean Sea. Gibraltar being in British hands, we fired them a salute, with no shot in the guns, and they fired one back. We sailed through the narrow strait dead true on course, with flags flying and all our redcoats lined up standing to attention, and I felt proud to be part of the ship.

It was strange to have a feeling like that. I had it again the next time we fired a salute, when we had sailed halfway across the Mediterranean, past the rocky coasts of islands whose names I didn't know, to join the fleet and our Admiral. I counted nine great ships scattered across that blue sea, and a few smaller ones, and when we had saluted one another, Lord Nelson came back aboard with Captain Hardy to take HMS *Victory* as his flagship.

Our Captain Sutton left us, with all the ship's company standing at attention and the bosun's pipe shrilling and the ship's band playing; off he went in the Admiral's barge to take command of the frigate *Amphion*, which had been Captain Hardy's ship. The men were sorry to see him go, because he was a good captain and Captain Hardy was said to be a strict man for discipline. But Nelson had chosen to have Hardy, and nothing mattered more to any of the men than the honor of being on the same ship as Horatio Nelson.

It was hard to believe that less than a year earlier I had hardly even heard of him.

When I was growing up, the only songs I ever heard were the lullabies my mother used to sing to the little ones, or the hymns in church. I still heard hymns, and sang them too, at the chaplain's service on deck on Sundays, but for the first time I discovered other music as well, in the forecastle—"fo'c'sle" for short—when the men got together just to be themselves. Three or four of them could play a pennywhistle, and one of the topmen had a fiddle and was really good. He would play hornpipes often, and some of the men would dance. And a few sang songs—sad songs usually, about their sweethearts, or some heartless girl who had forsaken them.

Jonathan Stead was one of these, to my astonishment; he had a warm, deep voice, and his mournful face made the sad songs seem even sadder. Sometimes he played a pipe between verses. It was strange to see big strong sailors sitting quietly listening to him with faraway looks and even tears in their eyes.

> *Here's adieu, sweet lovely Nancy,*
> *Ten thousand times adieu.*
> *I'm a-going round the ocean,*
> *To seek for something new.*
> *Come change your ring with me, dear girl,*
> *Come change your ring with me,*
> *For it might be a token of true love*
> *While I am on the sea . . .*

One day after supper when I was on the edge of the crowd listening to Jonathan singing in the fo'c'sle, Tommy the cook's assistant came looking for me. He pulled at my sleeve to draw me to a quieter corner, beside the black iron carronade that fired the biggest cannonballs of all the ship's guns. His shiny face was less cheerful than usual.

"Sam," he said, "we need you help."

I blinked at him. "Me?"

"You remember catchin' the rats?" Tommy said.

I grinned. The rats had been my only small triumph in my days as cook's boy, aside from the chickens—well, in fact because of the chickens. Rats are a major pest on board ship, second to nothing but the maggots and weevils in ship's bread. When food supplies are loaded into the ship's hold before a voyage, there are always a few rats inside the bags of vegetables or fruit who have nibbled their way in from the warehouse or some farmer's barn. And once they are on board, they live down there in the hold with the stores and they eat, and breed. When I was working in the galley, somehow a few of them made their way up to my chicken coops, and began stealing eggs and even chicks. The cook had a cat called Pricker, but she was fat and spoiled and paid the rats no attention. So I had rigged snares, the same kind I had always used on the farm to catch rabbits, and one after another I had caught seven big rats. The cook had been so impressed that he didn't yell at me for a whole week, and the chickens were left in peace again.

I said to Tommy, "I remember."

"Well, they back," Tommy said. "And they big trouble. They ate a whole pan of slush two days back, and Mr. Carroll got so mad at me—"

Now I was close, I could see that one of his eyes was puffy and half shut. I was furious.

"He hit you!"

Tommy looked down. "Well, he was mad. And there wasn't no rat to hit." He looked up at me again, through the good eye. "Sam—come set you traps, huh?"

So after supper next day I slipped down to the galley, after cleaning away the spoons and platters and helping stow the mess table. Tommy had found me some wire and I had a spool of yarn from my uncle, and the cook willingly gave me a hunk of cheese—elderly cheese, stinking now as it molded in the Mediterranean heat. But the stink was fine for catching rats. I set snares all over the galley, and next day we found them all full of dead rats—except for one snare with a horrid bloody foot in it, where the desperate rat had gnawed through its own leg to get away.

I did this three days running, with help from Stephen. By the third day I found he was selling dead rats to some of the crew, who carried them off and roasted them for supper.

"Roasted *rats*?" I said.

Stephen shrugged. "They're fine fat rats, raised on the ship's vittles same as us. Fresh meat, Sam. You should skin them, like you used to skin your rabbits. Use those sailmaker needles and thread to make a ratskin jacket. Or a hat to cover your own little rat's tail."

He gave my new pigtail a tug, and I punched him, and we rolled around thumping each other and laughing, until Tommy came shushing us because the cook, full of grog, was taking a nap.

But the rats kept coming. They were multiplying in the hold faster than we could catch them. Then they started attacking the chicken coops again, and Mr. Carroll said Mr. Burke the purser was getting worried about the amount of his stores they were gobbling up.

HMS *Victory* had been at sea for eight months now and the stores needed replenishing anyway. It was spring, and the weather was changing; you could feel warmth in the air, and the seas were less often stormy. We were sailing east, on our endless crisscrossing of the Mediterranean Sea, waiting for the French fleet to put out from Toulon. At supper one night Mr. Hartnell said he had heard we were to put in at the Maddalena islands, off the northern tip of Sardinia, to take on fresh water and meat, and a stock of the onions and lemons that the Admiral had us eat to keep off the scurvy. Two days later, sure enough, we were anchoring off the rock-edged harbor of a green island, with a great scurrying aloft as the men lowered sail, and a great treading of feet round the capstan as we dropped anchor. There was no talking or shouting at times like that: only the shrilling of the bosun's calls, the shouted orders that went between them, and the creaking and rattling of rigging and chain and sails.

Then names were called for three crews of men to go ashore in the boats to pick up supplies, and to my astonishment I was among them.

"You're so lucky!" Stephen whined. "Why you? It's not fair!"

William Pope said, "I'll tell you why. He's young and he's strong and they know he won't run away, because of his uncle. And because he's an enlisted man—if he deserted, he could hang."

I'd had no thought of deserting, but hearing this certainly encouraged me to banish the thought if it ever came into my head.

William gave me his shoes to wear that day, though I was used to going barefoot. "Those rocks will be sharp," he said. "And wear your jacket in case the weather turns dirty."

"Yes, mother," I said.

William said, "And bring back my shoes or I'll beat you silly."

I was put in the same boat as one of the quartermasters, Arthur Lessimore, a big, grizzled fellow who was a friend of my uncle's. He put me beside him because he had a mind to teach me to row. The oar was far too heavy for me to move on my own, but I did learn the motions. And it was a good thing he was beside me when we climbed up onto the rough stone jetty in the harbor, because to my surprise I had a hard time keeping my balance. I wobbled about and clutched at Lessimore's arm, and he laughed at me.

"Have to get your land legs back, Sam. Me too. It's a long time since we walked on something that didn't move."

Maybe that was when I began to realize that I was truly becoming a sailor.

Once we were in the scrubby little town, where everyone on the island seemed to be jabbering away at us in Italian with something to sell, I found that Lessimore was in charge of buying live poultry, and that I was there to help him. The chicken boy again. I was soon busy tying hens together in bunches by their legs, with yarn looped so as not to hurt them. Most of them came out of the cart of a skinny old fellow with a red scarf tied round his head, who spoke no English. His face was as lined as a raisin, and he had very few teeth. Lessimore had just enough words of Italian to be able to speak to him, and I discovered that the Italian word for chicken was *pollo*.

Two little dogs were scuttling round under the wheels of the old man's cart, runty creatures with no tails, dirty white and as skinny as he was. They never made a sound, though they bared their teeth at any other dog that came near them. They didn't bother me but they were always under my feet—I had to kick at them to get past. But then a wagon stopped beside us to unload sacks of vegetables for the ship, and both dogs dived underneath it and disappeared for a long time. The poultryman didn't call them; he paid no attention. After a while I noticed that they were back, and that one of them was carrying a dead rat in its mouth.

This got me to thinking.

"Mr. Lessimore," I said, "look at that!"

Lessimore was sweating like a pig from helping load sacks into the boat. That was ordinary seamen's work, but he was a good-hearted fellow and just wanted the job done. He straightened up and looked at the dog.

"Ugliest creature I ever saw," he said.

"But it's a ratter. And we have a swarm of rats on board."

"We have cats for that, Sam," said Lessimore wearily, so I decided to keep my ideas to myself.

"What's the Italian for dog?" I said.

"Cannay," said Lessimore. "Let's have those chickens, smart now."

But I had sixpence in my pocket from our rat sales, and a piece of ship's bread that William had given me, and there was something I wanted to do with them. It was only when we were back in the ship's boat, pulling toward *Victory*, that Arthur Lessimore realized what I was holding under my coat. The ugly little dog was cuddled up against me quiet as could be, partly because it was hoping for more bread and partly out of astonishment at finding itself cuddled by anyone in the world.

"Are you mad, boy?" said the quartermaster. "Over the side with it, this minute!"

I knew he had a soft spot for me though, so I tried to sound as young and trusting as I could. "Oh please sir, let me keep it. Just to give it a try against the rats. Surely Mr. Burke would be much obliged if we could save his stores."

Walter Burke, the purser, was not the most popular man in the ship because pursers were famous for watering the wine and giving short weight—but his gratitude could be a valuable thing.

Arthur Lessimore gave a snort; I wasn't sure whether it was agreement or laughter. "Keep your jacket closed," he said.

And the dog must have understood the value of not being seen or heard, because he was still and quiet as a mouse all the way over the side of the ship and down into the hold. That was where Tommy and Stephen and I took him. Then I let him go. We stood there, watching. He nosed about for a bit, and then he slipped gently behind a barrel—and there was a rattling flurry of movement back there, and a high screech, and out came my Cannay, dragging a rat almost as big as himself.

He did this five times in succession, and then we took him and the rats up to the galley and showed them to the cook.

"I'll be damned," said Charles Carroll, and he went to the steep tub where the salt port was soaking, hooked out a lump of it, set it on a chopping board and hacked off a piece the size of his fist. He dropped the pork back into the tub and gave the piece to Cannay, who was watching him, quivering. I can't think of anything nastier than raw fatty salt pork—it was terrible even after it was cooked—but the little dog wolfed it down, looked up at us and, having no tail, wagged his rear end.

The cook's fat tabby cat Pricker came sidling round into the galley and saw Cannay. Her tail went straight up in the air and she hissed at him.

"Best hold your tongue, cat," said the cook. "And take lessons from this little bugger."

And so an ugly little Sardinian dog came to live on board HMS *Victory* for a while, to join the pigs and goats and sheep, chickens and ducks and cats—and the green parrot belonging to the topman Richard Bacon, which could make a noise like a drumroll, squawk out "Splice the mainbrace!" and sing a shanty that would have made the chaplain have a fit. Cannay spent a lot of his time in the hold, and I spent a lot of my time cleaning up after him, but the rat population shrank to a much lower level. Even the cat Pricker, inspired or jealous, began catching a few.

Our income from dead rats went down, but it was worth it to be rid of the certain sight of those pairs of red eyes gleaming out from the dark corners of the hold. Cannay was wonderful. And I think the Navy gave him the best time of his life.

Though I was working some of the time with Mr. Smith and the sailmakers, I was not in the end written down as his apprentice, because it turned out that my hands weren't big enough to handle the needles and leather palms that have to be used in working with canvas. I could only sew lighter stuff. I was just too young for proper sailmaking—even though I had already grown out of the clothes issued to me when I first joined the ship. Lieutenant Quilliam had stopped in front of me at one Sunday morning inspection and poked his cane at my shirt-sleeves, which now ended halfway up my forearms.

"Sam Robbins," he said, "you look like something out of the poorhouse. Go to the purser for a new set of slops—I will write you a permission."

"Aye aye, sir," I said reluctantly—for the clothes you were issued by the purser would be charged against your pay, on that distant day when the ship came back to port and its crew was paid off. So for a while I looked very smart with new blue trousers and two new striped shirts, though they needed a lot of washing because I was still looking after the poultry when Mr. Smith had no need of me. We no longer had to muck out the pigs, though; they had all been eaten.

Autumn came again, and more storms with it, and one tossing day Colin Turner fell down a hatchway and broke his arm. It was bound to a piece of wood and he was back about again within a week, but the surgeon forbade him to use the arm— and that was a piece of luck for me, because Colin was powder monkey to the number six gun on the lower gundeck, and they put me there in his place. I was delighted. Now I really felt I belonged to the ship.

We lived our whole lives with and around guns, on the *Victory*. She bristled with cannon, those three decks of them, with the biggest guns down on the lowest of the three. Two decks below that, under the waterline and safe from cannon-shot, was the grand magazine where all the powder and shot was kept. You couldn't get anywhere near the magazine without permission, and there were guards to keep everyone away; one accidental spark there, and the whole ship could blow up. Even a rat gnawing through a gunpowder bag and leaving a little explosive trail could be a disaster, so the magazine walls were lined with copper to keep the rats out.

When the drum beat to quarters—calling us to battle stations—everyone on the ship had his own precise duties. We had seen no real action on *Victory* since the day I came aboard, but gunnery practice was endless; the Admiral wanted us ready. The men knew he was sick to death of waiting for the

French Navy to come out of Toulon harbor and fight—but when they did come, he was bound and determined to win.

Up to now my job had been to run to the galley at the call of the drum, to help Mr. Carroll and Tommy put out the cooking fires, and then to stay there, after filling buckets with fresh water to be set beside each gun during the action for the men to drink. Other people would be filling tubs with salt water pumped from the sea, to put out fires, wetting down the sails, scattering wet sand on the decks. The whole ship was stripped for action in a sort of whirlwind, mess tables and officers' furniture whisked out of the way, the cannons released and run out, and all the gunners' supplies put in place. Most of the men stripped to the waist too, and tied scarves round their ears to keep out at least a bit of the tremendous roar of the guns.

Before my first practice, Jonathan, who was part of the number six gun crew, told me I should strip too now that I was part of active duty.

"Your shirt gets in the way," he said. "And the surgeon's happier without it."

"The surgeon?"

"If you take a musket ball in the chest, a piece of your shirt likely goes in with it. The surgeon may cut the ball out, but if he don't see that bit of cloth, the wound goes bad and you die."

"Oh," I said shakily, and ever afterward whipped off my shirt the moment the drums began beating out *Hearts of Oak* for quarters.

Down on the lower gundeck there were thirty great black cannon, each firing a thirty-two-pound ball that could smash a huge hole in the side of an enemy ship, or knock down a mast with a direct hit. It took fourteen men to load and fire each gun, and my job was to keep them supplied with the gunpowder that fired the shot. Behind each cannonball they loaded a cartridge, a flannel cylinder as long as my forearm, packed tight with gunpowder.

Jonathan handed me a long wooden box. "This is your cartridge case," he said. "Your salt box, they call it. You carry the cartridge in there at all times—otherwise, a spark hits it and it blows up and takes you with it."

I was listening very hard, half excited, half scared.

"I am the powderman of the crew," he said. "I stand here by the breech, I give you the empty case, you run like the clappers down through the hatchway to the orlop deck. Each hatchway has wetted blankets hanging, against sparks. Dick Bacon is the next man in our line, he'll be waiting for you there with a new cartridge from the magazine, in its case. You swap cases and you run back here with the new one and give it to me. Got that?"

"Aye aye, sir," I said.

"I give you the empty case, you run again—the gun is loaded, it fires, and if the recoil caught you it would smash you to bits, but by then you are running back for the next cartridge—and so it goes. Understand?"

"Aye aye, sir."

"And wear shoes. A powder monkey with a broken toe is no use to anyone."

"Thank you, Jonathan."

But I wasn't prepared for the crashing thunderous reality of gunnery practice, the stinking black smoke filling the decks and hatchways, the flurry of boys and men running to and fro for cartridges and shot, the murderous backward leap of the recoiling guns. At every practice there was some sort of accident, a limb broken by a jumping gun, a terrible burn from powder exploding. And this wasn't even real action.

The gun crews loved gunnery practice though, and before long so did I. Each crew competed with the next, for speed and accuracy, and the officers watched us like hawks and toured the gundecks, cursing and threatening us and urging us on. I ran and jumped and dodged, I wanted to be the quickest powder monkey on the ship.

Once I came skidding up to my gun with a full cartridge case just at the moment when the bosun's pipe shrilled for a cease-fire, and the shouts rang out *"Belay there!"*—and I found myself facing gold braid and blue jackets as I cannoned full into two officers. I was so full of excitement that I was still laughing with delight, even as I raised my head and looked up into the strong stern face of Captain Hardy.

I stood frozen, clutching my salt box, but before the captain could say a word there was a laugh from the smaller man beside him, and a voice, soft and rather light, with a faint country accent:

"That's the face of my fleet, Hardy, look at the joy in it! What's your name, boy?"

I looked at the pale face and the pinned empty sleeve and I knew it was Vice-Admiral Nelson. And he was smiling at me.

I touched my fingers to my forehead in a panic, and my voice came out in a squeak. "Sam Robbins, Your Honor."

"Well, Sam," he said, "you are part of the fastest crew on this deck, and good luck to you all. An extra tot for these men."

Our crew gave a hoarse ragged cheer, and the officers went away. And that was one of the very best days of my whole life.

In the middle of our second winter in the Mediterranean, the French fleet did move out of Toulon, and for weeks we sailed to and fro through rough seas searching for them, only to find in the end that a gale had driven them back into harbor.

"They'll be out again," said Mr. Smith at the mess table, whacking his piece of bread on the table to break it and knock any maggots out. He nodded his head wisely. "You mark my words. It won't be long. Bonaparte wants to invade England, he'll want all his ships in the Channel."

My uncle said, "The carpenter heard Mr. Quilliam say Spain has declared war on us again."

"Spanish Navy never yet beat ours," Jonathan said.

"Surely not, but Boney has the whole of Europe on his side now. He has the pride of the devil, that one—crowned himself Emperor, took the crown right out of the hands of the Pope and set it on his own head!"

Mr. Smith squished a piece of boiled turnip onto a bit of bread. He said, "Such big thoughts, and him not but a small little man."

Jonathan said, "Our Admiral is a small little man too, but a lion inside."

"God bless him!" they all said, and raised their mugs and drank to Nelson, even though they had only the tail-end of the Mediterranean red wine they called black strap—since all the rum had long ago run out. There was nothing in my mug but an inch of stale water, but I drank his health too.

And before spring was out, a frigate came bowling over the sea to tell us that the French had run for it, and were out of Toulon. We went all around looking for them, and then two weeks later word came that they had gone west and were out past Gibraltar, in the open sea. Everyone knew that the Admiral must be wild to get after them. But we were shut in the Mediterranean and we hadn't the right wind. Slowly we worked our way west against light headwinds, and you never saw so many seamen whistling to the air, or following other private spells, to try and summon up a levanter, the strong easterly wind that would help us on our way. But none came.

We reached Gibraltar, and cast anchor with the wind still foul. That did give pleasure to the officers and men who were allowed ashore (I was not one of them this time) while we took on fresh water and supplies, and sent all the ship's linens ashore to be washed in fresh water for the first time in many months. Off went the boats to the great rock, full of eager men.

Hugh Portfield and I were on deck, scrubbing clean the chicken coops that would soon have new birds in them, and with us was a seaman pumping up seawater to wash them off. I never did know his name; like Tommy, he came from Jamaica and spoke that singing English. We were all working away when suddenly there was a great bang as one of the cannons on the upper gundeck went off. The smoke from it puffed out over the water. We all stopped, staring.

Figures were moving about on the quarterdeck. I could see the Admiral's starred coat, and his cocked hat with the green shade that sheltered his eyes. Then a flag was run up at the fore-mast, a white rectangle on a blue ground.

"What's that?" said Hugh.

"Blue Peter," said the seaman. "The flag for setting sail. They're calling the men back from shore."

The ship was growing busy. A midshipman came running toward us. "Finish that up, lads, smartly now! Get those coops below." He paused, and gave us a quick grin; for a moment he was just a boy, like us. He said, "The Admiral's got his wind!"

As we scurried about, I could see Admiral Nelson pacing impatiently to and fro while the ship's boats gradually began to creep back toward us from the shore. Sure enough, the few sails hanging high above our heads began to droop, and then rattle, as the wind changed and picked up. The bosun's pipe shrilled, and men ran to the rigging and began to climb.

And before the day was half over we were sailing out into the Atlantic Ocean, and all the ship's linens were left behind.

The French had sailed to the West Indies, and we were chasing them. In spite of our haste in leaving Gibraltar we had fresh water on board, and fresh meat and vegetables, which brightened everybody's life considerably. And the men who had been moaning about having to drink wine in the Mediterranean were cheerful at the prospect of our taking on West Indian rum. All that our Admiral was thinking about, we knew, was sailing as fast as possible to catch the French.

And we were for sure sailing fast. It was a wonderful sight, that great ship with all sails spread, thundering along with a following wind and white water foaming round the bow. The rest of the fleet had a hard time keeping up with us.

"Trade winds, Sam," said William Smith. "They blow all

year, northeast to southwest across the Atlantic, and give a smart run in this direction. Coming back, it's a different matter."

It was one of my days for sailmaking work, and we were up on deck, working in the sun. The others were cutting a spare staysail out of a huge roll of canvas. Because of my too-small hands Mr. Smith used me only for sewing thinner stuff; this time I was mending the bosun's hammock. I was being very careful; for a ship's boy, doing a job for Will Wilmet the bosun was a bit like working for God.

I looked out at the blue sky, scattered now with puffy white clouds. The air smelled of salt, and of the tar between the planks of the deck, that was soft enough now to mark bare feet. "Richard Bacon said we would see flying fish soon. Is that true?"

"Not up here, lad," Jonathan said. "They skim the surface, like little birds. I was in a cutter once and they came right onto the deck—not onto big old Victory, though."

"You'll see wonders," Mr. Smith said solemnly. "A bird called a pelican with a great bag under his bill, to hold his fish. Huge hairy spiders as big as your hand. A nut as big as your head. White beaches, green palm trees, fish all the colors of the rainbow. And the sun shines all day, in the tropics."

Jonathan tugged hard at the canvas, inching it off the roll. "But then a great black squall can come up fast as lightning and take your masts off, if you're not careful. And offshore from those pretty white beaches there's a million mosquitoes and sandfleas to drive you mad with itching. If you haven't already died of yellow fever or malaria, or the bloody flux."

"Jonathan Stead," said Mr. Smith, "God gave thee a beautiful voice and a very dark soul."

"I speak true, is all," Jonathan said. "Pass me the shears. And consider that before we reach those palm trees, we are like to be in action, which this poor lad has never seen."

I said, "I hear a lot about it. The men tell such tales, all blood and guts."

"All true," Jonathan said.

Mr. Smith said gruffly, "Well. We are at war."

Somewhere across the afterdeck a terrible shrieking noise started up, hurting my ears.

"What's that?"

"The grindstone," Jonathan said. "They'll be working to sharpen everything that has a blade—cutlass, tomahawk, pike, dirk, axe. When the fight comes hand to hand, we have to be able to kill those Frenchies fast, before they can kill us."

We sped along for another two weeks, and the sun grew warmer and turned us all brown-skinned, except for some fair fellows whose skin would only redden and blister, and who had to keep their shirts on however hot it might be. Our gun crew did well at exercises, and we were all in good spirits until one day when Stephen came to grief.

He deserved it, I suppose, though he was never a bad fellow. He just could not resist pocketing something now and then from the galley; it seemed to him a natural part of his job. I had given up warning him, and nobody ever caught him; the other boys simply knew that if Stephen wanted you to roll his hammock for him, or wash his shirt, he would pay you with an orange or a piece of cheese. I think even Mr. Carroll turned a blind eye to it, probably because he behaved the same way himself.

Every Sunday, after crew inspection and divine service, the captain made a formal inspection of the entire ship. So at the start of the day, before the drums beat to muster and we all trooped on deck, Lieutenant Quilliam would make a whirlwind tour of the ship with two midshipmen to make sure nothing would be found wrong. All we boys stood to attention on the upper gundeck as he strode past; he wore white gloves, and ran a finger along a beam here or a box there to check for dust.

He passed us by without comment, and we all felt a quiver of relief. But one of the midshipmen behind him paused in front of Stephen. It was Oliver Pickin, tall, tanned and confident, and he leaned past Stephen and reached into his kitbag.

I don't think it can just have been an impulse; I think he knew. He called to the lieutenant, and he held up an orange.

Lieutenant Quilliam looked back. He hesitated, but he was clearly in a hurry. "See to it, Mr. Pickin," he said, and kept on going.

Stephen was standing stiffly to attention.

"Is this yours?" said Pickin.

"Aye, sir," Stephen said. "Cook gave me it, please sir."

Pickin smiled. "We'll see about that," he said, and off he went in his smart Sunday midshipman's uniform, taking the orange with him.

And of course Mr. Carroll had not given Stephen the orange, Stephen had stolen it—and thievery is a bad crime in the Royal Navy. He was sentenced to two dozen lashes.

Boys were not flogged as men were, with the cat-o'-nine-tails, because it would have killed them. I had seen several floggings aboard *Victory* and I don't like to think about them; each time, the man's back was turned to a bloody pulp and he was not a normal person again for weeks afterward. Those floggings were done in high ritual style in front of the whole crew, but Stephen was beaten below decks; he was bent over a cannon, tied down, and given two dozen hard strokes with a cane by a bosun's mate, with all of us boys lined up to watch and all the midshipmen too. Lieutenant Quilliam was there in command. It was awful. Stephen looked so small, bent over that cannon.

They took him down to the surgeon afterward, because he was bleeding badly; he said the vinegar that was put on the cuts to help them heal hurt almost as much as the beating. Hugh and I tried to do all his work for him for days, and of course he couldn't sit down. I would hear him crying softly in his hammock at night, and I wished bitterly that I had been able to stop him pinching things from the galley. He did stop, after that. At least I think he did.

You always had to remember, in the Navy, how close you were to disaster. I don't just mean close to death in battle. The topmen who raced up the rigging were always one step away from a fall that would send them hurtling down either to the deck, which would break their necks, or into the sea, where they would drown. So were the lookouts, and the midshipmen when they were sent aloft. Danger was everywhere; you could fall overboard in a storm, you could be crushed by the recoil of a cannon or a shift of cargo in the hold. And if ever you lost your temper with an officer, however badly he had treated you, you could be hanged.

I was saved from that, one terrifying day.

Stephen and I were crossing the deck on our way back from an errand for the cook. I was walking a little behind him, as I always tried to do now to keep him from hurt; his wounds were still raw, and anything banging into him was anguish. Even wearing his trousers was painful for him.

Ahead of us was a group of midshipmen with their quadrants, practicing taking a bearing, as they regularly did with the captain or another officer to instruct them. There was only a little room to pass them, so we took care, but as we drew level someone cannoned into me, knocking me hard against Stephen's back. Stephen cried out in pain.

I turned round, and saw Oliver Pickin looking down at us, smiling. "Poor little Stephen," he said. "Does it still hurt then? Are we having a bit of trouble sitting down?"

He had done it on purpose, and for the second time. I hated him, that minute; it was like a noise in my head. I could think of nothing but that I had to punch him. I felt my fists clench, and I know I began that quick backward turn before you pull back your arm to hit someone—but from behind me a hand took hold of my arm.

And that light, faintly accented voice said, "Mr. Pickin, in this service a man who has suffered punishment has paid his dues. It is not the act of a gentleman, let alone an officer, to make reference to it. I should be obliged if you would apologize."

If I hadn't already realized that it was the Admiral, Oliver Pickin's face would have told me. He had flushed even darker than his tan, appalled and terrified.

"Aye aye, sir," he said. His eyes went to Stephen, and he said stiffly, "I beg your pardon, Mr. Sabine."

The hand let go of my arm, and I looked round and saw that thin brown face, beneath the green eyeshade and the cocked hat.

"Sam Robbins, is it not?" said Admiral Nelson. "You are a good friend, Sam. Now go about your business."

And we saluted him and ran, and I knew that he had saved my life.

Molly

❧

IN ENGLAND

FOR THREE DAYS, MOLLY AND KATE AND THE GRANDPARENTS ZIGZAG ACROSS LONDON WITH SMALL DONALD, DOING ALL THE things they used to do in city summers. They visit the London Zoo and give Donald a ride in a cart drawn by a llama, and watch the seals and the penguins show off as they are fed. They chug up the River Thames in a boat to Hampton Court, and have tea. They go one afternoon to the Globe Theatre, built as a replica of Shakespeare's own Globe, and see a wonderful production of *The Tempest*. Molly is very impressed by the acrobatic young actor playing Ariel, even though the program tells her he comes from North Carolina.

She is still in a state of aching happiness at being home again.

Next day it is raining, and her grandparents are very apologetic, as if the lack of sunshine were a personal failure on their part.

"Such a shame, when you only have this week," says Granny irritably. "It's *August*. I don't know what the weather can be thinking of."

This seems to Molly such an endearingly English remark that she crosses the room and gives her grandmother a hug.

"Thank you," says Granny in surprise, and hugs her back. Then she studies her, with the expression which is becoming familiar to Molly; a mixture of concern and affection and caution, as if Molly were a small fragile object which might shatter. They all look at her like that, Granny and Grandad and Mum. It makes her feel she has to appear sturdy and bright and brisk, at all costs, though inside she feels torn in half. The thought of going away from this place again looms ahead like a huge black cloud.

Kate comes into the room, looking relaxed. "Donald has gone to sleep, thank the Lord," she says. "I'm going to put a load in the washing machine. Why don't you three go to a movie, at that little cinema down the hill?"

"What an excellent idea," Grandad says. "Then we'll come back and I shall take us all out to dinner, including Donald." He begins flipping through the newspaper, looking for the film listings.

Granny says, "And you must have a think about what you'd like to do tomorrow, Molly dear. It's your call, as they say. Anything you fancy."

This is too good a chance to miss, so instantly Molly brings out the request she is now longing to make. "The thing I'd most of all like," she says, "really really most, is to go and see Lord Nelson's ship. HMS Victory."

"Good gracious!" Granny says.

Out of the corner of her eye Molly sees Grandad's head go up. She knows he used to be in the Royal Navy, long ago.

Kate says, looking slightly stunned, "She's been reading a book about Nelson—right, darling?"

Molly suddenly finds herself not only bright and brisk, but fluent. "It's in Portsmouth Harbour," she says. "I know it's a long way. Too far for Donald. Maybe Grandad and I could go. And you two could have a mother and daughter day, and Granny can do some bonding with Donald."

Grandad is smiling. "An old friend of mine is a guide on board the Victory," he says. "He will be so astonished to see us, I can't wait to see his face. Molly, my love, that's an excellent idea. Portsmouth trains go from Waterloo, I believe."

Next day, Molly and Grandad catch the Portsmouth train from Waterloo Station: a handsome blue and white train, with orange and red doors. It has a voice, a metallic but soothing female voice which speaks from the ceiling and tells them that this is the 9:08 train for Portsmouth Harbour, and adds a list of the stations at which it will stop on the way. Molly feels a twitch of excitement as they begin to move. She is sitting next to the window. Grandad is beside her, reading *The Times*.

Gradually the tall buildings of London fall away as the train hums along, and Molly is looking at a landscape that she has not seen for a long time; the familiar rows of small brick houses, with tiled roofs, and clay chimneys with television antennas attached to them, and outdoor drainpipes running down from each roof. Blackberry bushes bloom along the edge of the railway track. It is a very ordinary English sight, but she looks at it with pleasure and affection. Fields slide by, green fields with sheep grazing in them.

Grandad folds *The Times* and tosses it onto the table in front of them. "Tell me why you want to see the Victory, Moll," he says. "What's this book you've been reading?"

So Molly eagerly tells him the story of going to Mystic Seaport, and the rain driving them into Mr. Waterford's shop, and *The Life of Nelson* that she bought there because he reminded her of Trafalgar Square and home. But even now, even to her grandfather, whom she trusts more than almost anyone in the world, she says nothing about Samuel Robbins's piece of Nelson's flag.

Outside, a little village flashes past, all thatched roofs and bright blossoming gardens.

"Oh!" Molly says in delight.

"Picture book," says Grandad, nodding.

"There are no villages in America," says Molly. "Not like that."

"I suppose not," Grandad says. "Mind you, we don't have prairies or cowboys or Rocky Mountains either."

Molly says, "There are no cowboys in Connecticut."

"Carl's house looks very agreeable, from the pictures," Grandad says mildly. "And you have a pretty room, yes?"

"Yes, I do," Molly says. "But it's all so different. Everything in America is too big."

Grandad rubs his thumb down one side of his beard, as she

remembers he always used to do when he was busy thinking. Watching him, Molly finds all her deep miserable homesickness crystallizing into an astonishingly simple idea. In a moment, she has suddenly found the answer to all the problems of her life. Why did she never think of this before?

She half-turns herself to face Grandad, and he looks at her small intent face and thinks: *what's coming?*

"Grandad," Molly says, "could you and Granny adopt me?"

He blinks at her. "Adopt you?"

"So that I could live with you. I wouldn't be any trouble, honest. My room is already there, for me to live in, and I could go to my old school on the Tube, and help Granny in the garden—and chop things up when you're cooking—"

Grandad can't smile at this, he is too appalled. "And what about your mother?"

Molly sees her wonderful idea lose some brilliance, as if a cloud had swallowed up the sun. In her heart she knows she could never leave her mother, but even so she persists with this sudden new dream.

"I'd see Mum for all the holidays," she says.

"Sweetheart—Kate loves you. It would break her heart."

"I don't think it would," Molly says doggedly. "She loves Carl too and she doesn't mind America. And she's got Donald. Looking after Donald is a fulltime job."

The train's metallic voice says, *"The next station is Havant. Please change here for Chichester and Brighton."*

"*Parenthood* is a fulltime job," says Grandad, reflecting that it is also lifelong. He is suddenly very concerned not just for Molly, but for his daughter.

"Please, Grandad," Molly says.

"We'll discuss it," he says cautiously. "We'll all discuss it. But today's mission is HMS Victory. Do you remember the Nelson bicentennial last year? Sea Britain, and all those celebrations? Victory won't be so crowded this year, with any luck."

So they both take refuge in a little talk about Horatio Lord Nelson, though still Molly does not say anything about her piece of the flag. Nor about the strange fragments of dream which have begun to haunt her at intervals, more and more often now, like surfacing memories she did not know she had. All she knows about these hauntings is that they are something to do with Samuel Robbins and HMS *Victory*, and that they are becoming more and more important to her.

They have stopped at Havant, which seems to consist of a very long platform and not much else. *"This train is for Portsmouth Harbour, and the next stop is Fratton,"* says the voice, and there is a little chirpy sound as they begin to move again. Grandad has taken hold of Molly's hand, and they are sitting together in silence, with her question about adoption hanging between them like an unexploded bomb.

As the train leaves Fratton, and sets off for Portsmouth and Southsea, a couple of chunky people in raincoats come stumbling through the carriage. They pause beside Grandad. "Excuse me, sir," says the man, in a strong Texas accent. "Do we take the next stop for HMS Victory?"

"Not the next one. You want the last stop, Portsmouth Harbour."

"The ship is right in the harbor, then?" says the woman.

Molly eyes them both with smug English superiority. *Typical American tourists,* she thinks.

"Indeed it is," Grandad says politely.

The Americans collapse into the two seats opposite, and the man looks at his watch. "Almost eleven o'clock," he says. "This train was due in at ten thirty-nine."

Molly says in her clearest voice, "Trains are late in America too," and Grandad surreptitiously smacks her hand.

"They certainly are," the lady tourist says amiably. Her husband says nothing, and Molly lapses into a private fantasy about his being banned entry to HMS *Victory.*

Raindrops begin to spatter against the windows of the train. When they arrive at Portsmouth Harbour they have to pull up their collars and set out into driving wind and rain, dodging puddles, toward the Visitor Centre. Molly is filled with excitement, but when they line up for tickets to see the *Victory* she is dismayed to find a person in a white gorilla suit prancing about and greeting the visitors. A gorilla? For Lord Nelson? Clearly everyone here is classified as a tourist, not just the Americans.

But she can see masts ahead, reaching up over the wet roofs. She tugs Grandad along, and a tall policeman in a rain-cape smiles at her impatience. "Straight along the walkway, m'dear," he says.

And there is HMS *Victory.* She is amazing, enormous, with three masts reaching up into the sky from the great bulk of the ship. Her sides slope outward, mustard-colored, black-striped, filled with square black gunports. Molly stands still, gazing up. The rain spatters her face, but she does not notice.

The wind is singing in the rigging: a wild, commanding, timeless noise.

Grandad looks at Molly's face, and smiles.

He leads her under the towering bowsprit, below the figure-head where carved cherubs support the royal coat of arms, past gigantic iron anchors suspended over the side. Molly follows him as if she were walking in a dream.

Grandad heads toward a square black entrance in the side of the ship, and Molly pauses, taken aback, feeling it shouldn't be there. But there it is, so she goes on, after him, into a dimlit space that he tells her is the lower gundeck. A sailor takes their tickets, and gives them a leaflet with a plan of the ship.

And Molly stands on board HMS *Victory*, looking, listening, feeling against all reason that she has been here before.

SAM

1805

We never did catch the French ships; all we saw of them, in the end, was a few planks floating in the sea. And I never did set foot on any island of the West Indies, though we passed by a lot of them, with their green-topped cliffs and their exotic names: Barbados, Trinidad, Grenada, Antigua. But I saw pelicans diving into the sea with their great bills pointed down like swords, and black man o' war birds slowly circling high, high up in the sky. And once when the lookout called in excitement down from the mast, out over the sea we all saw a glittering jet of water go up into the air, again and again, from a whale, spouting.

We did pause once to take on supplies, but then turned east

again and chased the French back across the Atlantic Ocean.

"Why did they come all the way across, just to go back again?" I asked at supper.

"Beats me," my uncle said.

Mr. Hartnell said, "There's talk that maybe they were drawing us away while they invaded England."

"No!" I said in horror.

"No indeed," he said. "Those talkers are wrong. There's the rest of His Majesty's Navy out there, to keep Boney off. But our Admiral is in a right old hurry—watch how he piles on sail every day."

So he did, too. And gun practice was regular even though it used up precious powder and shot, and so was practice with the cutlass and the pike. Even us boys, for whom a cutlass was too big and heavy, were trained to use a dirk or a knife.

"For see you here," said the bosun's mate, knife in hand, teaching us the quickest way to kill a man, "if the Frenchies are swarming over the side and one comes at you screaming, the only thing that matters is for you to kill him before he kills you. So you holds your knife like *this*, and you sticks it in *there*, and you pulls it upwards and then out again—"

This was the one part of the training that made me feel sick, but I knew he was right. I had been in the Navy for more than two years now, I had turned twelve and then thirteen; I had grown a hand's breadth in height and I had a real sailor's pigtail that my uncle plaited for me every Saturday. But we had never fought a battle; I had never been in action.

Action was coming soon, that was for sure. I was half afraid of it and half excited.

I loved HMS *Victory*. When first I was pressed into the service and began to learn about the sea, I was puzzled by the way the men talked of a ship not as "it" but as "she." But now I understood. A ship is not just a floating house, she has a character, like a person. She may be well-behaved or cranky under sail, she may answer swiftly or lazily to the helmsman at the wheel, she may be tight and dry or leaky-wet. When you lie awake in your hammock at night, you can hear the ship talking all around you; she creaks and squeaks and groans, all the time, and up aloft, her rigging sings in the wind.

And because we lived inside the ship and were therefore in her protection, I felt that in a way she was also our mother.

I missed my own mother bitterly, every moment, in the beginning. Even now, after two years, I thought of her very often, and wondered over and over how she was, and how my sisters were, and even my father and my brother. I wrote letters, whenever there was a chance for mail to go back to England, and my uncle had them sent with his own letters to my aunt Joan, hoping that she could somehow reach our house. Though my mother could not read or write well, and my father not at all, I hoped that by now my sisters would have learned. But I never had a letter back, though once my aunt wrote and told Uncle Charlie that she had visited and found them all well. That was kind of her, for it was a hard journey. It was a long grief to me to have no way of hearing from Mam.

Perhaps that lack was one of the reasons for my love of HMS *Victory*. She was always amazing, this small city of people in one floating wooden frame, but there were two moments above all when she was truly beautiful. The first came when we were to leave after we had been at anchor, or at any rate not under way, with all sails furled. There would be that wonderful order from the captain or the admiral on the quarterdeck: "All hands make sail!"—followed by the high calls on the pipes of the bosun and the bosun's mates. Hundreds of feet thundered over the deck, hands reached for the rigging, then came: "Away aloft!" and the seamen flung themselves up the shrouds of the three great masts, maintopmen competing against foretop and mizzentop to see who could get there first. I held my breath as I watched them on that dangerous upward rush, every time, half longing to be one of them, half terrified of the risk of a fall.

Then came: "Trice up! Lay out!" and the tiny figures aloft would swarm out along the yards, till the masts and rigging looked like a tree in autumn thronged with migrating birds. And the last order was the one I waited for with most delight: "Let fall, sheet home, haul aboard, hoist away!"—for then suddenly, to a chorus of moving ropes and blocks and beams, all the sails of the ship would drop, rise, fill, all at once, billowing out to catch the wind. And *Victory* under full sail carried four full acres of canvas—held up by those twenty-seven miles of rigging, cared for and mended and remade by my uncle and the other ropers.

My other favorite moment came when the ship was indeed under full sail, cutting through the ocean, rising and falling in the swells, with a bone in her teeth, as the men said—meaning the white spray she threw off on either side of the bow. I saw neither of these favorite moments in my first year on the ship, being trapped below decks by my duties. But now that I was older and no longer owned completely by the cook, I was on deck far more often, happy in the smells of the sea and the spray, that were so much more agreeable than the multifarious below-decks stinks of the ship and her men.

And I knew that someday, when I was bigger, I would work and beg and pray to become one of the topmen running up those masts. This was where I lived my life, now; this was where I belonged.

When I said this to my uncle Charlie, he smiled rather sadly and shook his head. "More power to thy young heart, Sam. As for me, I shall be back on land to my Joan the minute I am able."

I could understand his feelings; after all, he was nearly forty years old. But none of us was close to being able to go home again, not yet.

Five weeks after setting sail from the West Indies we were back once more at Gibraltar, and then we sailed north, to meet Admiral Cornwallis's Channel Fleet one evening in August, off Ushant. It was early evening when we reached them; we fired our salute across the sea and it echoed round the fleet like thunder. All the ships of our squadron stayed there with the fleet except *Superb*, who sailed on with us to England, and three days later we put Admiral Nelson ashore at Portsmouth Point after two and a quarter years at sea.

Even then, only the officers were allowed to leave the ship—and only some of the officers, at that. None of us men and boys was allowed to leave at all. Britain was at war, and the Navy would not risk giving any of its seamen—specially those who had been unwillingly pressed—the chance of deserting. So although women were allowed to visit the ship, and my aunt Joan came and brought presents for Uncle Charlie and me, I had no hope of going home to see my family. And I knew that even if my mother had been able to visit Portsmouth, three days by coach from our home, my father would never have let her go.

But it was good to hear the seagulls wheeling and crying overhead, off the Hampshire coast. Nowhere else in the world, it seems to me, do the gulls call with the same voice as they do over the waters around England.

Less than a month after we came home, we set sail again. On the 15th of September 1805, very early in the morning, the Admiral's barge was lowered over the side from its place on the main deck, and its crew of seamen dressed very neat in white trousers and striped shirts pulled away toward Southsea, which is a part of Portsmouth. There they picked up Admiral Nelson from the beach, which the men said was thronged with hundreds of people cheering and wishing him well; and with Captain Hardy he came back to us, looking very splendid in a blue coat shining with the stars and ribbons of all the awards he had won.

I had just a glimpse of him as he came over the side, with the bosun's pipe shrilling and the marines all lined up in their red and white uniforms, and I felt proud and frightened at the same time. My uncle and all the other men in our mess had said that we were off to fight the biggest of all the battles against Bonaparte; that the Admiral knew the whole French and Spanish fleets were gathered in the Spanish harbor of Cadiz, and he was taking us down there to blow them out of the water.

"And mark you," Mr. Hartnell had said in a sad deep voice, looking I thought straight at me, "a lot of the men on this ship will be blowed out of the water at the same time."

So we sailed south, and by September 27th we were off Cadiz, joining the British fleet that had been waiting there under Admiral Collingwood—though we fired no welcoming salute this time, nor got one, because our Admiral had forbidden it. The sea was filled with great ships of the line; it was a grand sight. For three days running we had their captains arriving at HMS *Victory* for dinners, one of them celebrating our Admiral's forty-seventh birthday, and there was an endless piping and saluting as they came aboard.

Captain Hardy had the ship's paint touched up, though whether that was for a birthday celebration I do not know, and because I was strong but light I was one of those lowered over the side with paint and brush, to hang over the waves trying to dodge the spray. The sides of the ship were broad stripes of yellow and black, and within the three yellow stripes were all our gunports, which had to be painted black with no black smears or dribbles. It was no easy job, hanging there sitting on a board with ropes strung through it and lashed round your waist. The worst danger was not of falling into the sea, but of catching the rage of Lieutenant Quilliam if you splashed yellow paint on a black stripe, or left a black toeprint on a yellow one as the sea swung you against the side.

The boat crews bringing the captains from the rest of the fleet told us that the other ships were being painted to match *Victory*'s pattern. Every ship had to paint its masts buff-colored as well, to make sure they looked different from the hooped masts of the French and Spanish fleets.

I said to Jonathan, next to me when we heard this, "Surely everyone can tell their ships from ours?"

He looked at me as you might look at a baby who calls a chicken a duck.

"This is for the thick of battle, Sam," he said. "A ship is just a ship if its colors are shot away."

But of course I had not seen battle, yet. I cannot tell you the difference that makes, in a mind, in a heart.

We sailed to and fro, out at sea off Cadiz, fifty miles out, watching the captains of our fleet come and go as the Admiral summoned them to HMS *Victory* to tell them his battle plans. I knew we were waiting for the enemy ships to come out of Cadiz harbor, but we were so far offshore that we couldn't see them over the horizon. All we could see were the distant sails of Lord Collingwood's smaller British fleet, between us and the coast.

"That's Nelson for you," said the captain of our gun crew, as we paused in one more mock drill. "He knows just where to sit so that the Frenchies can't see him. They can see Old Coll's fleet, but they have no idea how many ships we have all told."

"But we can't see them either," I said, and then wished I had not spoken, because I was only the powder boy.

He answered just as if I was a man, though; we were a team, he was treating us all alike. "He's got fast little frigates like Euryalus watching Cadiz," he said. "If the frigates see the enemy come out, they clap on sail and signal Coll, and he signals us. And we chase!"

And that, in the end, was what happened, on October 19th in the morning. I was below decks, off duty, stealing a visit to Hugh to help him feed the chickens. Even though I no longer worked for the cook at all, I liked to be reminded of the farm and home. But suddenly the bosun's pipes shrilled out above our heads, calling all hands, and heavy feet came clattering down the stairs. And I knew, with a sudden hollow feeling in my stomach, that this was the first step on the way to battle.

The poor chickens and their coops were snatched away in a squawking flurry, and a great banging and hammering began. Partitions and hatchways and even ladders were lashed up high or cut completely away, to leave as much space as possible for us to run out and fire the guns. I was sent to help roll hammocks and carry them up to the deck, to be stuffed into the netting along the sides of the ship—something we did every day, but extra important now as a protection against splinters and shot. Other men were loading furniture from the officers' quarters down into the hold.

On we sailed, all this while; all through that day and the next, with the sea choppy and the wind sometimes fierce. We took our hammocks down to sleep in them, and then put them back again. At night, blue lights tossed on the horizon, and flares lit up the clouds; they were signals from the frigates, telling our Admiral that they still had the enemy ships in sight. And by the morning of October 21st, a warm hazy morning with the sun trying to shine, we saw them too. They had put out from Cadiz, on the west coast of Spain, not knowing that we were sailing up from the Strait of Gibraltar to catch them— twenty miles off the rocks of a cape called Trafalgar.

Now we were really sailing toward battle. Some of us were sailing toward death. I was not thinking about this when we were eating our breakfast, because for once we had neither the nasty burgoo nor our imitation coffee, but an issue of fresh bread, cheese, butter and beer. But Jonathan sat beside me, alternately sharpening his knife on a leather strop and using the knife to shred his hard lump of cheese.

"Young Sam," he said, "if I go overboard, you are to take my kit for your own. Our messmates are my witness. The bag is strung up by that beam there."

"Go overboard?" I said.

"There's no nice ceremony in battle," Jonathan said. "A dead man has to be flipped over the side, out of the way." He looked at me with the nearest thing to a smile I had ever seen on his face. "But you will have to learn to play my pipe," he said, "for I'll not have it wasted."

"And another thing," said my uncle Charlie, on his other side. He pulled a ring off his finger, leaned past Jonathan and took hold of my hand. The only place the ring would fit was over my left thumb. "Take that to thine aunt, Sam, if need be," he said. "With my love."

I was getting really frightened, for the first time. Up on deck, drums were beating, and the bosun's mates' pipes rising in command. "I'm just as likely to get killed as you are," I said.

"True," Jonathan said. "But I have a feeling about that. I think you will come through. Here, sharpen your knife." He tossed me the leather strop.

I heard myself say something that until now had been part of my private nightmares. "I'd rather be killed than have my arm or my leg cut off."

"No you wouldn't," said Jonathan. "If Horatio Nelson can lead us all with one arm and one eye, anyone can do anything." He tapped his mug of beer on the table and held it up to the other men, raising his voice, "To the Admiral, God bless him!"

"Bless him!" they rumbled—and then the pipes changed pitch to call us all up on deck. There was a rush to stow our things and hang up the table, and up we ran, to find the crew cheering. Out on the horizon was the long line of great ships of the French and Spanish fleet, and up in our rigging was a line of signal flags.

I could see Admiral Nelson on the quarterdeck, in his blue coat with all the bright stars and medals on it. He was looking up at the signal, and I think he was smiling.

I looked at the string of flags and said urgently to anyone who would listen, "What does it say?"

A big grizzled seaman beside me said, "He has signaled the fleet: *England expects that every man will do his duty*."

And across the waves from the British ships sailing behind us came more cheers, clear and defiant, carried on the wind, carried into the teeth of the destruction that was waiting for us ahead.

Molly

~~~

ABOARD HMS *VICTORY*

LIKE A VAST ROOM THE GUNDECK STRETCHES BEFORE THEM, DIMLY LIT BY LANTERNS. THERE IS MORE SENSE OF SPACE THAN Molly had expected. Great black cannons line the side of the ship, the nearest one higher than her head, and she can just make out the shapes of another row on the other side. There is wooden planking under her feet, and over her head. She sees wooden buckets, racks of cannonballs, coils of rope.

"Each of those balls weighs thirty-two pounds," Grandad says. "These were the biggest guns, down here. When they were fired, the recoil sent them rushing backward to where we're standing, hundreds of pounds of iron like a missile, and you had to keep clear or you'd be squashed. See those huge thick ropes threaded round each gun? They caught it when it recoiled, so that it wouldn't go crashing backward right across the deck."

Molly's ears ring; for an instant she hears faraway thunder and feels a quivering under her feet. Then it is gone.

She says to Grandad, almost accusingly, "You've been here before."

"I certainly have," Grandad says. "I'm a devoted member of The Nelson Society—we know a lot about this old ship. So I'm your personal guide, Miss Molly, at least until we find my friend Joe. This is what they call a 'freeflow' day on Victory, when you can wander about alone instead of being part of a guided tour."

Molly says, "That's good. Tours are for tourists."

"We're not tourists?"

"Of course not. We belong." And as she says it, she feels somehow that the ship agrees.

Grandad leads her up some ladderlike steps to the next deck. Again it is lined with cannons, poking their deadly noses out of the side of the ship through holes in square Plexiglas windows. Rain beats against the Plexiglas.

"Gunports," says Grandad. "These guns are run out—that means they're sticking out, ready to fire. But there was none of that glass in Nelson's day. When the gunports were open, the rain came in, and the spray, and everyone was wet most of the time. This is the middle gundeck, twenty-four-pounders, twelve men to each gun. And that huge round wooden thing behind you is the capstan. It goes down to the deck below, and when the ship was about to set sail, two hundred and sixty men on the two decks pushed it around to wind up the anchor line. A marine beat a drum to keep them in time—*heave . . . heave. . . .*"

Faintly in Molly's head a drum beats, tapping out a tune she does not know, and yet thinks she has heard before. She is feeling very strange, as if another world were leaking into her own.

"So many guns," she says.

"And more yet," Grandad says. "This beautiful ship was a killing machine, I'm afraid. But look up there—it's Nelson's own cabin."

And there it is ahead of them, through a polished doorway: the Great Cabin of the Admiral. But it is filled with a group of tourists, among them the two Americans from the train, and Molly hangs back. Grandad looks at her questioningly.

"No, thank you," she says.

"Are you sure? It's Nelson's cabin—isn't he your reason for being here?"

"Well, sort of," Molly says. "But not just him." She is looking at a notice on the wall. It says:

HMS VICTORY AFTER 157 YEARS OF SERVICE WAS PLACED IN 1922 IN HER PRESENT BERTH IN THE OLDEST DOCK IN THE WORLD, AND RESTORED TO HER CONDITION AS AT TRAFALGAR

She thinks: *everything around me is just the way it was. . . .*

Up they go again. Everywhere the steps are so steep that she cannot imagine what it was like to climb them when this ship was at sea. Now they are on the upper gundeck, the topmost of the three, lined on both sides with twelve-pounder cannon. All these guns give Molly a sense of foreboding; she tries not to look at them. She pays more attention to the hutches labeled FOR HENS AND ANIMALS, and the sick berth, where canvas cots with straw mattresses inside them hang from the beams overhead. On a table there are wooden bowls and mugs, and spoons made out of bone, all looking as if they were waiting for someone to come and use them.

At the front of the berth, three steps up, inside a door, she finds a special little toilet for the sick men. Watching, Grandad says, "All the healthy men had to go up into a very bouncy place called the heads, with holes in a plank hanging over the sea, and do their business there. Not much fun, eh? It was up this way—"

And he takes her up more steps to the forecastle, the outdoor deck high in the bow. Wind and rain lash at them, and they zip up their coats. The wind is humming in the rigging; the sound fills Molly's head. She thinks: *it's a sound there is no word for; it's the sound Sam and Nelson heard.*

The wind sings in from the other world, joining then and now.

Clutching their collars, they stumble the length of *Victory's* deck toward the stern, past the towering mainmast, past the ship's boats that look to Molly bigger and sturdier than Carl's sailboat. Pointing upward, Grandad shouts in her ear, "That's the poopdeck, where Nelson was standing when he was shot."

Molly nods, but stays below the poopdeck, and finds the door to Captain Hardy's cabin. When she read her book she liked the sound of Hardy, Nelson's loyal friend who kissed him good-bye before he died. Inside the cabin, there is a plain cot right next to a twelve-pound cannon, and then an astonishing room looking as if it were in a town, not on board ship. There is a handsome leather-covered sofa and a shiny table, with two chairs with carved backs, and two with red velvet seats. Two English ladies in raincoats and plastic headscarves are gazing at them.

"Cor blimey, that's posh, i'n't it?" says one to the other.

"Must have been nailed down," the second lady says.

Out they go to the windy deck again, Molly and Grandad, with the singing of the rigging all around them. The deck is almost empty. Grandad huddles himself into his coat; Molly gazes up at the towering masts. Before she left America she had copied out and learned by heart the older of the two inscriptions in the front of her book, Emma Tenney's inscription:

This the most precious possession of my father Samuel Robbins, his piece of the flag of HMS Victory *on which he served as a boy at Trafalgar. Given into my safekeeping as a girl, before his last voyage from which he did not return. May God bless my dear father and his Admiral. . . .*

Remembering it, she knows now that she is trying to reach out to the boy Sam Robbins, to touch his hand in the past. And that he, for reasons of his own, is reaching out to her.

"Go in out of the wind, Grandad," she says. "I won't be a minute, I'll catch up with you."

Grandad looks at her doubtfully.

"Truly," Molly says. The wind blows her hood across her face and she pulls it aside to peek at him. And since he is deeply concerned about her state of mind, and knows the necessity, sometimes, of solitude, he nods his head and goes to the hatchway leading below.

Molly stands there in the whipping rain, listening to the wind, seeking any feeling or hint of long-dead Sam, and wondering what he felt when he was here. She thinks too of her father, who fell out of the sky into the ocean, to die where Sam must have died on that *last voyage from which he did not return.* Misery flows into her mind, but she does not know whether it is brought by the cold rain or by her own condition of life.

The misery grows, it clutches at her. She finds a strange metallic taste in her mouth, and she is gripped by a wave of wretchedness so strong that she hears herself give a sharp groan. At the same time she thinks she hears an echo of a voice.

. . . Insolence! A bar in his mouth for three days! . . .

She looks round nervously, but there is nobody about to hear her, or the voice, if it was there; the rain is keeping them all belowdecks.

Then for an astonishing moment, as she looks up at the grey sky and sees the humming, singing ropes of the rigging, suddenly the sense of misery vanishes away and she feels a lightness, a joy simply at being on the ship. It is as if the strange sound were embracing her. There is an ominous quality to it, but it brings more pleasure than fear. She finds herself wishing that the ship were sailing; longing for it to break free from its last long home in Portsmouth Harbour and sail out into the waves.

She says experimentally to the air, "Sam?"

But of course there is no answer, and she goes to the hatchway and climbs down out of the rain, and finds Grandad waiting. When he sees her, he reaches out his arm to give her a hug.

Down they go again into the depths of the *Victory,* following the route marked out for visitors. Here and there, groups of tourists cluster around a guide posted to answer any questions they may have. On the upper gundeck, a sailor guide with a bald sun-browned head is pointing at a very long curved piece of wood: "This is the elmtree pump," he is saying. "It would bring up twenty-five gallons of water a minute, for washing down the decks or fighting fire."

For an instant Molly thinks she hears a big creaking sound, and the rhythmic whoosh of water—then it is gone, and she and Grandad are moving on past an older sailor who is telling another group, with gloomy relish, all about flogging and the making of a cat-o'-nine-tails. "Or if you were a boy," he says, "they'd thrash you with a cane instead. You'd be bent over a cannon—that was called kissing the gunner's daughter."

Molly feels a flick of horror, and hurries Grandad back down to the middle gundeck, with the great capstan, and hammocks hanging between the guns. "A hundred and forty-two marines slept here," another guide is telling a cluster of visitors.

Grandad says, "Here's the cook's galley, for their one hot meal of the day, about one o'clock. Two bells, in the middle watch. I forgot to tell you about bells."

But Molly isn't listening. Something is making her stare closely at the fire hearth and the tiled floor around it, and the big iron stove. Something here makes her feel close to Sam.

She lingers by the galley. It's as if she can feel a blast of heat, smell strange smells, hear sounds of bubbling water . . . and voices. . . .

. . . Everything out of this galley comes straight back, or you get a thrashing. . . .

Grandad says, "Are you all right, Moll?"

"I'm fine," she says with effort. "I'm fine." But she is not fine at all; she is caught in a haunting.

She follows him down, down again to the lower gundeck, where she sees tables lowered between the cannons. They are set with wooden dishes and wooden spoons, and samples of ship's bread, which are flat brown wheels looking as if they too were made of wood. There is a press of tourists down here; Molly can hear languages she thinks are French, German and Swedish, and others she cannot recognize. She feels oddly glad that they are there, as if they were a protection.

Grandad leads her down another set of ladderlike steps; the spaces are growing smaller, the ship darker. Something is making her drag her feet. *Not yet,* something is saying.

"This is the orlop," Grandad says. "Funny word, isn't it? Dutch—means 'covering.' It's the last deck above the hold, and the grand magazine where they kept the gunpowder and shot. We're below the waterline here, so the enemy couldn't fire into the magazine and blow everybody up."

Molly's ears are singing, her eyes blurring; she sees a jumble of cables, of netting hung from walls, of swinging hammocks. She moves slowly through the murk, feeling as though someone were pushing her away, trying to keep her from coming down here; as though someone were trying to protect her from a peril or distress or pain. In the almost-dark, she finds herself looking down into a kind of pit, filled with barrels and black metal lumps lying on what looks remarkably like a stony beach.

She hears Grandad saying cheerfully, "We're right at the bottom of the ship here—that's ballast, in the hold. Pig iron and shingle. And stores of course, barrels of water and meat—and over here, come—"

She follows, slowly, blindly.

"—the grand magazine—see the copper on the walls, to keep the rats out. If they nibbled through and left a little trail of gunpowder—BOOM! Anyone who came down here was searched, to make sure he had nothing that could cause a spark. And the barrels of gunpowder are padded from each other by sheets of leather, look—"

A voice from the murk says hesitantly, "Commander Blake?"

Molly looks up in surprise; she has never heard Grandad called a commander before.

Grandad is grinning broadly. "Joe!" he says.

A sailor comes forward out of a dimly lit corner: an old grey-haired man, Molly sees, though perhaps not so old as Grandad. He is wearing the navy-blue uniform of the guides, and he is holding out his right hand, and smiling.

"It was the voice," he says, "I could never forget that voice," and he seizes Grandad's hand and starts to shake it. "I'll be darned," he says. "Why didn't you tell me you were coming?"

"I believe in surprises," Grandad says cheerfully, and the two of them stand there shaking hands and beaming at each other until Molly thinks they will never stop.

Finally Grandad remembers her. "This is my granddaughter Molly," he says. "Moll, this is my old friend Joe Wilson. Radio operator, retired."

Joe Wilson reaches out to shake Molly's hand too. Her hand disappears for a moment inside his, which is very large.

"I was in the Navy with your grandfather, a long time ago, Molly," he says. "In the nineteen fifties, aboard a cruiser called HMS Bermuda."

Grandad says, "Have you had any word of . . ." and they are off on a tennis game of reminiscence, these two old shipmates, digging out of their memories the names that have been buried there since their youth. Molly lets them go through Nobby Clark and Peely Robertson, but then she can no longer bear the anxiety that is growing inside her head. She has to get away. She touches Grandad's arm.

"I'm just going up to the orlop deck again," she says. "I shan't be long."

Joe Wilson says, "I'd come with you, but I'm on duty down here. To stop people falling into the hold."

"Come straight back, sweetheart," Grandad says.

"I will."

"Look across from the top of the hatchway," Joe Wilson says, "and you'll see where Nelson died."

"Thank you."

But when she has climbed the ladder she keeps away from that side of the ship, because it is full of eager visitors crowding the low-roofed space. She is listening for something, though she does not know what. She knows only that she has to be on her own.

She slips away into a dark space with beams low overhead, and a table set out with two-hundred-year-old surgical instruments, and she finds black carved wooden columns facing her, and padlocked doors leading to tiny cabins, with iron gratings. Nobody else is here; they are all over there listening to a sailor telling them how Nelson died.

Noise is beginning to grow in Molly's ears, a rumbling, a roaring; it grows and grows and fills her head, thunderous, pouring in from the past. Desperate to get away from it, she looks wildly around and sees a cabin that has only a half-door, topped by a kind of shelf not quite as high as her waist. Hastily she hauls herself over it, and stumbles past some big storage bins into a second cabin beyond. Gasping in panic, with no one to see her, she falls into the dark little room and curls up in a ball on the floor, with her hands over her ears.

SAM

21 OCTOBER 1805

It was near the middle of the day and the air was hot down on our gundeck. I was sitting on a coil of rope with Stephen, who was now powder monkey to the next gun in line. We were waiting, waiting, keeping our balance as the ship pitched on toward the enemy. The massive black guns on our deck were to be double-shotted, loaded with twice the amount they usually fired.

"England expects us to do our duty?" said Andrew Scott a little peevishly to Jonathan. "Of course we'll do our duty, don't we always?"

"He knows that," Jonathan said soothingly—though he had

to say it loud too, for all of us had scarves bound round our heads and over our ears, against the noise that would swallow us when the firing began.

"Tha heard what he said about my notch," said George Harris, our gun captain—a big man, with massive shoulders browned by the West Indian sun. He ran a finger over a V-shaped scar he had cut into the surface of the gun carriage, and I ached to have been there when he was cutting it, as I had ached for the last hour after hearing the story. Earlier, I had been sent down to the orlop deck, to check yet again my route to the next man in line from the magazine, and while I was gone the Admiral had passed by our gun. With the marine band playing cheerfully up on deck, he was touring all the gun crews, and he had come up behind George as he was cutting into the wood, the men told me. George had leapt to attention, stiff and straight, dropping his knife with a clatter.

"What's this, George Harris?" said Lieutenant Quilliam, at the Admiral's side.

"A notch for each great British victory, Your Honor," George said. He pointed to the line of dark notches carved over the years into the old gun carriage. "I want this one done now, in case I'm not here to do it after."

Nelson had laughed. He sounded really happy, they said, as he always did before a battle. "You'll make notches enough in the enemy's ships," he said, and he clapped George on the back with his one arm, and moved on down the row of guns.

"I *wish* I'd been there!" I said now, again—but then all our heads went up, for somewhere out on the sea there was the deep sound of gunfire. Stephen and I jumped to our feet, and he ran back to his gun.

"Old Coll's reached them!" Andrew said. Word gets around a ship fast; even down on our dark gundeck we knew that the French and Spanish fleets were drawn up in a long line and that we were launching a double attack, one led by *Victory* and the other by Lord Collingwood's *Royal Sovereign*.

The rumbling and thumping came closer over the sea. We were all wound tight with waiting: sweating, bare-backed, some men rhythmically chewing tobacco, some laughing together, some quietly praying. The noise grew, until we could hear shouting up on deck; then there was a crash right overhead, as from somewhere a first shot hit *Victory*. Orders were shouted down to us to change the shot for our first broadside from double to single; the rest of the gun crew swung into action and I scrambled to keep out of their way.

It seemed like an age before the order came to fire. All the time through the gunport and the nearest hatchway we were hearing the mounting thunder of cannon, the horrid whine of shot passing overhead, and the crashes as cannonballs struck the ship. Up on deck, in the smoke and the roar, enemy fire was shredding our sails, smashing our spars, killing and wounding dozens and dozens of our men. Battle under sail is not like a prizefight, with two men hammering each other from the first moment to the last. It becomes so in the end, but before that, it is a long slow matter of sailing your ship into danger, enduring heavy fire, until you are in the right place to have all your guns at once smash away at the enemy.

And at last that moment came. There was another crash

overhead, the biggest so far—it must have been the shot that brought our mizzenmast down—and the whole ship shuddered. But above the cries and screams from the main deck we heard: "Make ready to fire!"—and we began. Even before our great gun first thundered and leapt back I was on my frantic way to fetch the next cartridge.

After that it was a blur of running and stumbling through the noise and smoke, to and fro between gun and orlop hatchway. And that space was made into the gateway of Hell, by something nobody could have warned me to expect.

You can be told about war, about death and wounds and pain, but nothing you are ever told will be like what you see and hear when it is all around you, real. On every run I made to fetch a new cartridge for the gun, I passed men on their way down to the surgeons in the forward part of the orlop deck; wounded men staggering as the ship rose and fell in the swells; screaming men being carried on swags of canvas, with great gaping wounds or with an arm or a leg shot away; silent white-faced men, unconscious, dragged by a desperate friend. And everywhere there was blood, bright red, running like water, dripping from one ladder step to another. Blood is slippery, you can slip in it, and then you yourself will bleed.

Once, swinging round with a new cartridge I found myself face to face with Oliver Pickin, his tanned face grey from strain or perhaps a wound, his white trousers splashed red with blood; he was holding in his arms another midshipman, George Westphal, bleeding dreadfully from a huge gash in his head. Pickin slipped, and nearly dropped Westphal on the deck.

"Sam—" he said urgently, jerking his head at a bucket of

sand beside me, and hearing him, the man who had just put a new salt box in my hand snatched it back for an instant so that I could upend the bucket and spill sand all round our feet. Then I was gone again, flying off with my cartridge, but leaving Pickin able to carry his burden safely in spite of the blood. Enemies who have a common enemy are made friends, I suppose.

The air was full of huge thunder and black smoke. Another explosion shook the ship, and she seemed to stand still. It was the shot that smashed our wheel and its tiller-ropes, so that a frenzied commotion began on the after end of our gundeck, where before long twenty men would be pushing the great tiller to steer *Victory*.

Out of our gunport, through the billowing smoke I caught a glimpse of another ship very close, and saw the flash of its guns. Then *Victory* must have slammed into her, for there was a thunderous crash like the world ending, and the impact lifted our huge gun up from its carriage and back again, and knocked us off our feet.

I was not thinking about anything now, nothing at all; I was just running. *Run, run, for a new cartridge; run, Sam, through the stinking smoke and the bloody sand. Run for your life, for your friends, for your ship, for your country, for your Admiral. . . .*

The ship lurched as all the guns on our side fired a broadside, and right after it came a tremendous explosion abovedecks from our huge sixty-eight-pound carronade, the biggest gun in the fleet. Then fast after that *Victory* lurched again as the starboard guns on the other side of our deck fired a broadside into another French ship. All was noise and smoke and destruction, deafening, terrible.

And then it was all suddenly even worse.

There was a blinding flash of light as a shot or a grenade crashed through our gunport, blowing up as it came. Everyone was flung about. Something hit my arm and spun me round to face the next gun in line, and in that instant I saw Stephen seem to explode. One instant he was a boy; the next, a bloody unrecognizable heap on the deck, beyond help, beyond hope.

George Harris's face came close to mine out of the smoke as he picked himself up. "Get down to the surgeon, boy!" he yelled, and I saw that half my right hand was shot away. For a moment I felt nothing, and then pain hit me like a fierce blow. Someone grabbed my arm and wound a rag round my hand, and down I stumbled over the sand, bleeding into it myself now, down to that part of the orlop deck that was the worst small hell of all in our pain-filled ship, being lined with the bodies of wounded and dying men.

The ceiling was low, down there, and the dark space was lit only by candles flickering in horn lanterns. I could just make out our chief surgeon Mr. Beatty, and two helpers, busy in one corner sawing off the shattered leg of a man who seemed to be mercifully unconscious. Closer by, the other surgeon Mr. Smith was sewing up a long gash in another seaman's back. His hand went up in the air with the needle in it and for a wild moment I was reminded of my mother sewing at home—but Mr. Smith was sewing a man's flesh, and like Mr. Beatty he was covered in blood, up his arms past his elbows and all over the long apron he wore.

I stood with a group of men waiting to be attended to, and another of the helpers looked at our wounds to see who should come first. When he came to me he made me drink a tot of rum, which stung my throat and made me fearful, because I had heard they gave you rum to dull the pain of having some part of you cut off.

"Way! Make way!" came a voice over the awful endless chorus of groans and pleas for help, and two men came slowly past me dragging a dead man by his arms. I looked down at the grey dead face as it went by, and I saw that it was Uncle Charlie.

I let out a great stricken cry. "My uncle! That's my uncle!" And though nobody in that terrible place had any time to care whether a corpse was a boy's uncle, one of the men carrying him glanced at me sorrowfully for a moment, out of black eyes in a dark brown face.

"Pray for his soul," he said—and they were gone, up toward the deck and the sea.

I don't know whether I prayed. I know I was sobbing, so hard that I barely noticed the pain of whatever the surgeon's assistant did to my hand, when it was my turn.

"Easy, boy," he said, bandaging me. "You're in luck—you lose two fingers but you keep your hand. Go sit over there, and hold thine arm in the air—the bleeding will stop presently."

So there I was, squatting in a haze of pain and misery, with the blood drying all over my bare chest, when they brought our Admiral down. And all my self-pity dissolved itself into shame.

That blue coat was unmistakable, with the bright stars and orders glimmering through the bloodstains, though his face was covered with a handkerchief at first. They said he had put it there himself, to hide himself from the men so as not to discourage them. From above us, there was continuous noise, as enemy shot crashed into our ship and the guns roared like angry animals.

They put him gently down not far from where I was. The chaplain Mr. Scott came to him, and very soon Mr. Beatty. In a little gap between bursts of gunfire I heard the Admiral say to him, "Ah, Mr. Beatty, you can do nothing for me. I have but a short time to live. My back is shot through."

Then another roaring broadside shook the ship, and figures gathered round him, and I saw and heard no more for a long time. I could think of only one thing. All the pain and loss, even the loss of my uncle, had retreated behind this one fact that was changing the whole world: the fact that we were losing Admiral Lord Nelson.

I must have been unconscious for a while after that. It was almost as if the world had become so bleak that I no longer wanted to be in it. But I was young and strong and my body had a will of its own. When I opened my eyes again, into the stuffy air of the orlop deck and the thunderous noise all around, I could see the Admiral once more. He was lying with a sheet draped over his waist and legs, and his bare chest was very white. He looked suddenly very small. The surgeons had gone to cope with the constant flow of new wounded men carried down from the deadly racket abovedecks, and for the moment only a small group remained round Nelson. Mr. Burke the purser was holding a pillow to prop up his shoulders and head. Someone was fanning the Admiral with a folded paper, and Mr. Scott was holding a cup to his lips from time to time.

I could just make out the Admiral's voice. "Fan . . . fan . . ." he was saying faintly. "Drink . . . drink . . ."

Mr. Scott tipped a cup that was clearly nearly empty, and looked around as if to ask for more, but nobody was close by. Next to me on the deck was a mug of lemonade someone had given me before I had passed out. I scrambled clumsily to my feet and carried it to him, in my good hand. Mr. Scott took it without noticing who was handing it to him, but I saw the Admiral's blue eyes move in my direction. He could only see out of one of them, of course, but he was looking at me.

He blinked, as if he were trying to focus, and he said softly, "Good boy."

Then Mr. Scott held the mug to his lips, and he sipped the lemonade.

Above the thunder from outside, and all the sounds of pain from around us, there was a sudden ruckus from the far corner of the orlop where Mr. Beatty was working on another amputation; a shriek, and several shouts. Mr. Beatty called loudly, urgently, "Mr. Benbow—I need you!" And the man who was fanning the Admiral jumped up, put the fan into my hand and ran.

So there I stood behind the Admiral's head, fanning him with my left hand, trying to ignore the throbbing of my right. I shall never know whether he knew I was Sam Robbins, or whether I was just a good boy, but that's of no consequence. It was the greatest privilege of my whole life, happening on the worst day of my whole life, and it went on for quite a while. Then the Admiral's steward Mr. Chevallier came running down to the orlop with tears all over his face, and thanked me, and took over the fanning.

The Admiral was dying.

I went back to my corner, and I cried too.

Molly

IN ENGLAND

AFTER MOLLY LEAVES HIM TO TAKE ANOTHER LOOK AT THE ORLOP DECK, THIS GRADUALLY BECOMES THE WORST DAY OF Grandad's long and eventful life. When twenty minutes have gone by, he goes to look for her. He cannot find her amongst the groups of absorbed tourists, so he enlists the help of his friend Joe Wilson. Several other sailors join in too.

After an hour, Grandad becomes worried enough to call Granny and Kate to find out whether they have heard from Molly; they have not. The search goes on. After two hours he calls again, and this time tells them about Molly's startling request to stay in England as an adoptee of her grandparents.

After two and a half hours, he begins to panic, and he calls the police. By this time every sailor on the *Victory* is quietly asking every visitor if they have seen a young girl of Molly's age and description, alone or with an adult. Joe Wilson is trying to pacify Grandad, who is distraught.

"She's got herself lost, that's what," says Joe Wilson. "They'll find her."

"She'd never leave the ship without me," Grandad says.

"Well, maybe she got hungry. Youngsters do, you know. Maybe she went looking for a snack."

Grandad says miserably, "Maybe she ran away."

"Now why would she do that?"

"She's desperately homesick. She's only here on a visit— her mother married an American and moved her to the States. This morning she asked me if my wife and I would adopt her."

"My word," says Joe. "What's her stepfather like?"

"He's a very nice fellow," says poor Grandad. "Molly just misses England. Where in the name of God has she got to?"

There are tears on Molly's face. Curled up in the darkness, she is caught in a grief that has come upon her from outside herself, swallowing her up, calling out echoes from the buried griefs of her own short life. Perhaps she is asleep; perhaps she is dreaming. She is so deep in misery, it is not clear even to her whether she is conscious.

A sailor guide approaches the half-door with a gaggle of tourists in tow. "This is the purser's daily issue room," he says. "Those big tubs would be full of foods he'd give out to the men—flour, dried peas and so on. You can see flour sacks lying on the floor beyond. That was the bread store."

"Listen!" says one of the tourists. "What's that?"

The sailor falls silent, and hears the sounds of muffled sobbing from the cabin beyond. He swings his legs over the half-door, goes in, and stares down at Molly, astonished and distressed.

Carl says into the telephone, "Kate, darling, slow down. Take a deep breath. Start again, now. She's disappeared from *where*?"

He listens unhappily to his frantic wife at the other end of the line. He has never heard her so frightened, and he is overcome by a desperate need to put his arms around her.

"She asked him *what*?" he says.

The frightened voice pours out of the telephone. Carl listens, frowning, thinking.

"I'm coming over," he says. "I'll get the first flight I can find. Hang in there, Katie. We'll find her. Call my cell the minute you hear anything. I'll be with you tomorrow. I love you."

He puts down the telephone and goes to look for Russell.

When the sailors carry Molly out of the inner cabin, and Grandad and Joe Wilson come rushing to her, it is still hard to tell whether or not she is conscious. Slumped on the deck with Grandad's arms around her, she murmurs odd words, and her eyes open and then close again. Somebody has called an ambulance, and before long there is a great commotion out on the dockfront and two large young paramedics come clattering down the ladder steps with a stretcher. Through the wind and the rain, Molly makes a dramatic exit from HMS *Victory* past an inquisitive crowd of visitors, and Joe Wilson insists on coming in the ambulance with Grandad because he is concerned by his old friend's deep distress.

They stare at Molly's pale face.

"Could she have fallen and hit her head?" the paramedic asks.

"There wasn't room," Joe says. "Lord knows how she ever got in there without someone seeing."

"I should have looked," Grandad says, anguished. "That second inside cabin—I didn't look."

"You did look. We all looked. She was tucked away as if she was hiding."

"Does she have any medical condition?" The paramedic is taking Molly's pulse again.

"Some petit mal epilepsy when she was small, but not for years now. And this is different."

"Well, they can do an EEG—that would show it." He looks down thoughtfully at Molly. "It's like she's in shock."

And that is what the doctor in the emergency ward at the hospital says too. She is puzzled. Everyone is puzzled. There is no sign of any physical damage whatsoever in Molly's small body, but she seems to have retreated into impenetrable sleep. She is tucked into a hospital bed to be observed for the next twenty-four hours, with an intravenous drip in her arm, and electrodes on her head monitoring her brain.

Grandad is in the waiting-room, trying to ignore a muttering television set. Joe Wilson sits beside him, to keep him company until Kate and Granny arrive.

Joe says hesitantly, "Did you have a son called Charlie? *Uncle Charlie*, she kept saying, *Uncle Charlie*, as if something terrible had happened to him."

"She hasn't got an uncle Charlie," Grandad says. "My daughter is an only child, and Molly's father had one sister who isn't married. There isn't even a family friend called Charlie."

"Oh."

They sit in silence, bent forward, elbows on knees.

"*Blood*," Grandad says at last, reluctantly. "Did you hear her say that?"

"Three times, she said it. Slow, like."

The clock on the wall above them ticks, barely audible. The television squawks a commercial.

"And that last thing, before she stopped talking. Did you hear that?"

"I did indeed."

"*Good boy*, she said. *Good boy*. Maybe they have a dog at home."

"And then she said, *The Admiral is dying*."

"Yes. She did."

Carl is in his study, calling his travel agent to cancel the hastily booked ticket to London. Kate has just telephoned him again, incoherent with relief that Molly has been found unharmed. She has assured him that they will be home in a few days and that there is nothing he could usefully do by crossing the Atlantic.

Russell is standing just inside the study door, fiddling unconsciously with the doorknob. It makes a regular squeaky rattling sound, like a rusty swing.

Carl hangs up the phone and throws an eraser at him. "Stop twitching! Molly's fine. They'll be back next week—maybe sooner."

Russell still hovers, his face serious. Carl is suddenly reminded of the way he would hesitate on the brink of words when he was an earnest eight-year-old, trying to summon up the courage for some kind of confession.

"Dad," Russell says, and stops.

"Well?"

"Moll had some kind of breakdown, on HMS Victory? That's Nelson's ship, right?"

Carl looks at him curiously. "Right."

"There's this thing that happened," Russell says. "I promised I wouldn't tell, but maybe it's . . . you remember she bought a book at Mystic Seaport?"

And he tells Carl about Robert Southey's *The Life of Nelson*, and about the finding of the piece of Nelson's flag. They go to Molly's bedroom and stare at the considerable collection of books on her shelves, and it turns out that Russell has paid more attention to Molly than she supposed.

"All her really favorite books are on this shelf," he says, peering close. "Yeah! Here it is!"

And Carl finds himself faced with the astonishing little piece of cloth in its primitive envelope, and with Emma Tenney's inscription.

This the most precious possession of my father Samuel Robbins, his piece of the flag of HMS Victory on which he served as a boy at Trafalgar. Given into my safekeeping as

a girl, before his last voyage from which he did not return.
May God bless my dear father and his Admiral.

"Holy cow!" he says.

Russell says unhappily, "I didn't think too much about it—but Moll was knocked sideways, I remember. She made me swear to keep it a secret. I wish I'd told you and Kate."

"Loyalty is better than snitching," Carl says. "Don't worry about it. I'm glad you told me now, though." He glances at Mr. Waterford's card, which seems to be marking Molly's place; then closes the book carefully and puts it back on the shelf.

"You don't think it's the reason this thing has happened to Moll?"

"No!" Carl says firmly. "Let's go get lunch."

But late that night, he goes back alone to Molly's room and takes down *The Life of Nelson* again. He has brought a magnifying glass with him, and he opens the book under the brightest light he can find. First he makes a note of the telephone number on Mr. Waterford's card, and then he looks intently at the book's remarkable inside page. He seems to be staring not at either of the two inscriptions, or even at the morsel of the flag, but at Emma Tenney's signature.

Donald has always been an amiable, cooperative baby. He is fast asleep in his stroller when Kate and Granny arrive with him at the hospital, and Granny keeps him in the waiting-room next to Joe Wilson, who has five grandchildren and is accustomed to babies. Grandad leads Kate down a buff-colored corridor to Molly's room, and as they tiptoe through the door Molly opens her eyes and gives them a sleepy smile.

"Hello, Mum," she says, and Kate is across the room in a flash, taking her in as close an embrace as the IV line will allow, pressing a damp cheek against her daughter's hair.

"Thank God," she says. "Oh Molly darling, thank God."

"I'm sorry," Molly says. Over her mother's shoulder her eyes meet Grandad's, and he knows she is saying it to him as well. He comes closer, and when Kate finally lets her go, Molly reaches out her hand to him. He gives it a squeeze.

"Do you remember what happened, Moll?" he says.

"Not really," Molly says. "Just waking up, and you being there. That was the good part." Her eyes grow distant, as if she were looking at something a very long way away. "But it was so dark—and so much noise—"

Kate says quickly, "Get some sleep, now. Don't try to think about it. We'll take you home to Highgate in the morning."

Grandad knows that they are faced with mystery, and that Kate and perhaps everyone will try not to press Molly to examine these few hours of her life during which she retreated from reality. He hears this in the voice of the doctor who admitted Molly to the hospital, who learns that Kate has arrived and comes to talk to them in the waiting-room before going off duty.

"Has she been under a lot of stress recently?" inquires the doctor gently. She is very young, with short blond hair, and stern black-rimmed glasses designed—Grandad guesses—to add *gravitas* to a very pretty face.

"We've moved to the United States," Kate says. "It's a big adjustment."

"When do you go back?"

"In a few days."

"Well, this wasn't any kind of seizure," the doctor says. "Physically she is just fine. Emotionally, who knows? Just keep an eye on her, as I'm sure you would anyway. If there are any other puzzling incidents you might want to try psychotherapy." She smiles at them, a conspiratorial English smile. "Plenty of therapists in America, I believe."

So all the conversation in Molly's family is of stress and emotional pressure, as they put themselves into two hotel rooms which have been booked by a helpful officer from HMS *Victory*. Joe Wilson had urged them to come home with him instead, but Granny said firmly but gratefully that it would be unthinkable to present his wife unexpectedly with three strange adults and a small baby. Joe Wilson, who has unlimited confidence in his wife, had looked disappointed.

Now in the hotel Granny's cell phone rings, and it is Carl, calling for a report on Molly. Granny tells him all is well and hands the phone to Kate.

And Grandad, who will not allow space in his life either for cell phones or for computers, goes outside into the Portsmouth night for a solitary walk. The rain has stopped and the wind has died down, leaving a dark, damp summer night.

Grandad walks slowly along the street, thinking of Molly's desperate plea to stay in Britain; thinking of the rapt expression on her face as she first gazed at HMS *Victory*; thinking of certain other moments on board Nelson's ship when perhaps she might have been hearing things that he did not hear. He thinks of Molly's father, his lost son-in-law, and of the way he died. He thinks of his own days in the Royal Navy, long ago, and of nights at sea, alone under a dark sky filled with blazing stars, when he felt a curious kinship with other sailors on that same sea from years or centuries ago.

And though he is appalled by the horror and grief Molly may have faced today, he thinks he can understand the mysterious four-hour vacancy that occurred in her consciousness. But he can hardly tell anybody, even his wife, that he believes his granddaughter may have witnessed the events of the Battle of Trafalgar, fought two hundred years ago.

Molly is back in her little room at her grandparents' house in Highgate, thinking about Sam Robbins. All day she has been very quiet, because she is in a stunned state of mind. When anyone has asked her questions about those hours on HMS *Victory* she has not properly told the truth—not even to Grandad. Although the whole thing is a painful blur, she is sure that she was feeling and hearing what Sam Robbins felt at Trafalgar. She does not think this was Sam's doing, even though she is also becoming convinced that he has somehow been trying to reach her ever since she found his piece of the *Victory*'s flag— or perhaps even before that.

She slips out of bed, pads over to the window and pulls the curtain open—carefully, so as not to make a noise. Through the zigzag pattern of the roofs around her she can see the night sky, brightened by the lights of London, with a few stars shining here and there. From the *Victory*, Sam would have seen a dark, dark sky with millions of stars.

She thinks: *he didn't want me to have to see the battle, he tried* to keep me away from it, but it was part of him so he couldn't. Like Grandad said, Victory was a killing machine. But it was Sam's new home and he loved it, because of Nelson. He loved Victory, and he loved the sea.

"*Good boy,*" she says aloud, finding the words in her head, and she wonders what they mean.

But one thing is clear as crystal in her mind now: she knows what she must do with Sam's piece of the flag.

She climbs back into bed and falls asleep.

It is their last day in London, a warm sunny day. Kate is in her bedroom, packing, and Molly brings her an armful of clothes from her own room, where she has been emptying the drawers of the bureau.

"Can I leave my sneakers here for next time?" she says.

"Of course," says Kate. She pauses, and looks at Molly, holding a sweater half-folded in her hands. She says, "Did this week make things worse instead of better?"

"No!" Molly says. She wrinkles her nose. "Well, just for a bit it did. I even asked Grandad if they would adopt me so I could stay here."

"I know," Kate says. She pauses, then gives Molly a wry grin. "I hope you've changed your mind."

"Mum!" says Molly. They look at each other across the open suitcase, these two survivors who know each other so well, and then Molly grins too. "I couldn't let Donald have you all to himself," she says.

"I love you too," Kate says. "Get out of here and make the most of your last day."

Molly goes downstairs. Granny is mowing the square of lawn behind the house, pushing the little whirring hand mower with contented precision. The sweet smell of mown grass drifts in through the open window.

Grandad is in the big kitchen-dining-room making scones for tea. Molly wanders in and watches him placing neat dollops of raisin-studded white dough onto the baking sheet. "There!" he says, sliding them into the oven, and he sets the timer.

Molly says, "Can we take some back with us tomorrow, if there's any left?"

"I made a double batch specially," says Grandad. "Make sure they get eaten fast, though—they don't keep for more than two days." He pulls off his apron, tangling it as usual with the glasses that he wears on a string round his neck. "I have something else for you to take back, Moll. It's over here."

He leads her to his big mahogany desk in a far corner of the room, and hands her a brown manila envelope. It isn't sealed. Molly opens the flap and pulls out a framed photograph.

"Oh!" she says. "It's Daddy!"

The picture shows a man squatting beside a tall model yacht, his hands raised to adjust its rigging. The water on which the yacht floats fills the whole background of the picture, as if it were the sea, and the man is looking back over his shoulder at the camera, laughing, saying words silenced forever by the click of the shutter.

"Taken at the Round Pond." Grandad says. "Seeing that boy there the other day reminded me. So I went through about six hundred pictures to find it, and had it enlarged for you."

Molly says, "It's wonderful. Thank you, Grandad." She puts

her arms round his neck, and his beard bristles against her cheek.

"You're welcome," he says, and kisses her. Then he moves her gently aside so that he can put his glasses on his nose. He picks up the photograph. "Take a look at this. I don't remember noticing it before, but the enlargement has brought it up."

He points to the stern of the tall graceful boat, as the timer buzzes from the stove, and Molly sees that a name is written there.

The yacht is called *Victory*.

SAM

JANUARY 1806

T HE SOUND OF THE DRUMS WAS LIKE THE BEATING OF A GREAT SLOW HEART. MUFFLED DRUMS, THEY WERE, WITH BLACK CLOTH over them. Everything was muffled that day, even the grey clouded sky. All of England was mourning the death of one man, and all the people of London were out on the streets leading to St. Paul's, and all the air filled with the slow beat of those drums and the unending slow march of thousands of feet.

Ten thousand soldiers were marching in procession, before and behind us, in that long step that they keep for funerals, with the hesitation in it that breaks your heart. Marines were marching too, and the cavalry regiments trotting their horses slow, with a soft jingle of harness, and artillery with horses pulling the creaking gun carriages. Every man of us wore black stockings, with black crepe on our hats, and black ribbons hung from the horses' heads. Over the beat of the drums, sometimes you would hear the wailing lament of a pipe band, like London weeping.

And there were we, forty-eight of us from the crew of his flagship HMS *Victory*, walking in pairs: forty-eight seamen and marines, with the senior men up front carrying our poor flag, the tattered white ensign that had flown from the masthead at the Battle of Trafalgar and been shot through and through. The men held it up sometimes to show it to the people lining the streets, and some said you could hear a rustle like the sound of the sea as hundreds and hundreds of men took off their hats in respect. Me, all I could hear was the drums, and the feet, and the boom of the minute guns.

Dozens of carriages creaked along behind us, drawn by more jingling horses, filled with noblemen and officers. Thirty-two admirals in full dress uniform there were at the Admiral's funeral, and a hundred captains. There never was a funeral like it, not even for a king. The Prince of Wales rode in his crested carriage just in front of the funeral car, a long gun carriage made to look like our *Victory*, with high prow and stern, and a canopy swaying above our Admiral's coffin.

With music and high words the funeral service lasted for hours, inside St. Paul's Cathedral. A great blaze of candles hung from the huge domed roof. At the very end, when the coffin was to be lowered into the ground, we seamen had been told to fold our ensign in ceremony, and lay it on the top. But when

Will Wilmet the bosun and three of the older men took up that shredded white cloth, Will gave a kind of sob—and suddenly all the men were reaching for our sad flag and it came apart, and they stuffed pieces of it into their jackets. And the coffin went down into the crypt, under the stone floor, forever.

He was a good man, Wilmet. He gave me a scrap of the flag for my own, afterward, outside the Cathedral, when we were gathering to march back through the streets of London without our Admiral.

"Here, young Sam," he said. "Here's a bit for you. Keep it till you die, and have it buried with you. Your own little bit of Nelson."

Molly

~≈~

IN CONNECTICUT

KATE, MOLLY AND DONALD HAVE BEEN BACK IN CONNECTICUT FOR THREE DAYS. IT IS DINNERTIME: A CELEBRATION DINNER, because Russell has passed his driving test. Kate has bought a chocolate raspberry ice-cream cake and decorated it with a Matchbox Corvette and one candle. Everyone has second helpings of the cake except Donald, who rejects his first helping but manages to smear a large amount of it over his face, hands and hair.

Russell says through a mouthful, "Jack would be pissed at missing this."

"Why isn't he here?" says Molly, privately very glad that he is not.

"He's gone. His doomy parents have sent him to some military academy in Virginia, and their term starts early. Oh by the way, he left you this."

Russell gets up and unpins an envelope from the kitchen bulletin board. Molly opens it cautiously. Inside is a card with a picture of an immensely ugly dog which has just fallen on its back after tugging at its leash, and the legend SORRY I WAS SUCH A JERK. The signature reads: *Until the next time—Jack Parker.*

"Well, that shows self-knowledge," says Kate.

"Say thank you for me, Russ," Molly says, because she knows that without obnoxious Jack, a great many things would not have happened.

"Okay," Russell says. "Dad, can I have the car tonight?"

"No," Carl says. "Today is cake. Don't push your luck."

Russell says, undeterred, "Well, how about tomorrow? I could drive us all to Mystic Seaport for that trip that got rained out."

Tomorrow will be Saturday. "Sounds good to me," Carl says.

"Count me out," Kate says. "Donald's going to a birthday party."

"A party?" says Carl. "He's eleven months old!"

"Everyone has a right to a social life," Kate says.

"Moll? Want to come to Mystic?"

"Yes, please," Molly says promptly. She longs to share her piece of flag with Mr. Waterford, and it surely shouldn't be too difficult to slip away from Carl and Russell for half an hour.

But it is.

They drive to Mystic Seaport the next morning, with

Russell at the wheel of Carl's car, and Carl, beside him, trying hard not to offer advice, comment or criticism. Molly thinks she sees Carl close his eyes as Russell accelerates past a truck on the highway, but she can't be sure.

They visit the ropewalk, which Molly finds oddly familiar even though she has never seen it before; they visit the cooper's shop, the shipsmith's forge, the sailing ship *L.A.Dunton*, the whaleship *Charles W. Morgan* and the tall ship *Joseph Conrad*. All the ships are considerably younger than HMS *Victory*, though Molly has the grace not to point this out. They eat lobster rolls for lunch at the Seaport café. Molly cannot escape. At length, even though they have already visited the Seaport's own excellent bookshop, she says, "I really want to go back to that bookshop we found on the rainy day. D'you mind if I go?"

"Let's do that!" Carl says enthusiastically.

"Sure!" says Russell. "That guy had some great magazines."

They get to their feet, and Molly is still trapped. She can find no reason at all for telling them she wants to go alone.

So they all three troop off to SHIPS AND THE SEA, and there at his desk is Mr. Waterford, small and grey-haired, smiling as if he were expecting them. Perhaps he is.

Molly says, "Mr. Waterford? I'm Molly Jennings."

"Hello, Molly," Mr. Waterford says. He raises his gaze to include Carl and Russell, who loom very tall in the low doorway, and Carl puts out his hand.

"Carl Hibbert," he says. "And Russell."

"I remember," Mr. Waterford says. "You've brought better weather with you this time."

Russell makes a beeline for the sailing magazines, and Carl

drifts off into the back room. When they are out of sight, Molly pulls her *Life of Nelson* out of the bag she has been clutching to her all this time.

Mr. Waterford looks at the book for a long time, peering first at the Edward Austen inscription and only then, with thin reverent fingers, unfolding the envelope to reveal the piece of the *Victory*'s flag and Emma Tenney's beautiful earlier handwriting. This he studies very carefully indeed, through a magnifying glass, and then he sits back with a kind of sigh. He takes off his glasses, and Molly sees those arresting grey eyes again.

"Astonishing," says Mr. Waterford. "Quite astonishing. The flag, yes, but also the story behind it."

Molly says, "Samuel Robbins. Is there any way to find out more about him?"

The grey eyes contemplate her. "That's the real reason you're here, isn't it, Molly? Not just to show the old bookseller your buried treasure."

"Well," Molly says. "Yes."

Mr. Waterford smiles at her. He puts his glasses back on, opens a drawer in his desk and pulls out a slim file of papers. "I did a little research after you e-mailed me," he says. "Look. Here is a list of the crew of HMS Victory at the time of Trafalgar—and here is Samuel Robbins. Classified as a ship's boy, aged thirteen, from London. But that's all anybody seems to know about him."

"I know things," Molly says. "I think I dream about him. It sounds crazy, but I sort of . . . hear things. Feelings, and words. Almost as if he's calling to me."

"Is that frightening?" Mr. Waterford asks.

"No—no, not at all. Only when he showed me frightening things—and that wasn't his fault, I think he tried not to." She stops, nervous that he will merely smile tolerantly, an adult listening to the imaginings of a child.

But Mr. Waterford is nodding, slowly. He picks up the book, cradling its spine in one hand as if he were judging its weight. He says, "One of the nicest things about being an antiquarian bookseller is the detective work you can do. This edition of Southey was published in London in eighteen hundred and ninety-seven. Sometime after that, Edward Austen must have bought this copy, and inside the front cover he stuck this homemade envelope. And wrote underneath it—" He looks down, putting his glasses back on— "*This fragment of the great man's life and death passed on to me by my grandmother at her death in eighteen eighty-nine*. That means he'd had the piece of the flag for at least eight years before he stuck it in the book. I wonder what made him hide it then—and hide it so thoroughly, sticking it down behind the endpaper of the book. Almost as if someone had told him to. So that it would be waiting."

Molly is only half listening now; she is not interested in Edward Austen, she only cares about Samuel Robbins. "And his grandmother Emma Tenney," she says, "she was Sam Robbins's daughter. When he grew up, he was her dad."

Mr. Waterford looks at her over his glasses for a moment, and there is a frowning crease between his eyebrows, as in a teacher contemplating a student who is failing to learn.

He puts *The Life of Nelson* on his desk and bends his angled desk lamp down to shine on the unfolded envelope that holds the piece of Nelson's flag. He nudges the fragment of cloth aside to reveal the signature written there. Then he gets down from his chair and beckons Molly.

"Come and look at this name. Through the glass. It might help explain why Edward Austen and you both chose this book."

It is a high, narrow chair, like a stool; Molly hauls herself up. Mr. Waterford puts his magnifying glass into her hand. He says, "Emma Tenney, you said? But look at the long tail of that first letter—and at the rest of the word—"

"Emma Jennings," Molly says, reading. She hears what she has said, and peers closer through the glass. "Not Emma Tenney. Emma Jennings."

"Like Molly Jennings," Russell says. He has come up behind Molly and is standing there quietly, looking over her shoulder. Molly half-turns, taken aback, but she is too involved in the matter of Emma to pay him attention.

Mr. Waterford says, "Suppose Emma Jennings had a son and a daughter. The daughter married a Mr. Austen, and had Edward Austen. The son would have had children named Jennings, and those who were boys would also have had children named Jennings. Suppose one of their descendants was your father."

Molly's face is a mixture of astonishment and delight and doubt. "Is that true? Could it be?"

Carl says, "Probably." He has come close while Molly was intent at the desk; he stands beside Mr. Waterford, towering over him.

"How do you know?"

"I made a phone call," Carl says. "I called your dad's father—your other grandfather."

"The one in *Australia?*" Molly's voice comes out in an incredulous squeak. She has never met her father's father; all she knows about him is that he left his wife and two small children one day long ago, sailed to Australia and never came back.

"Steve Jennings," Carl says. "Lives in Perth. Old and weird and doesn't like talking. But once he figured out I was harmless, he did admit there was a family story that his great-great-great-grandfather had fought at the Battle of Trafalgar."

He is looking at her, this tall confident stepfather, with a kind of nervous hopefulness, like a dog who has brought some well-meant offering but is prepared for rejection. Molly looks round at Russell and sees the same uncertain expression on his face too.

"You knew all this before I came back," she says to them both, and to Mr. Waterford. "You all talked to each other, but you didn't tell me."

Carl says, "You had such a hell of a week over there. I thought you had enough to cope with."

Molly thinks about this for a moment. Then she slips down from Mr. Waterford's stool-chair, puts her arms round Carl's waist as far as they will reach, and presses her head against his chest for a long moment. Only Russell can see the loving relief on Carl's face.

"We're all guilty of secret-breaking," Carl says. "Russ told me about your book, your mom gave me the phone number . . . we were worried, Moll."

"I know," Molly says. She takes her head out of his chest and looks at Russell.

"Fink," she says.

"Sure," says Russell cheerfully. "But how about it—you're Samuel Robbins's great-great-granddaughter! Or maybe a couple more greats in there."

Molly nods her head slowly. Out of all the strange sensations she has had, over the past two weeks, what she is feeling now is perhaps the strangest. It is such a mixture of things; she cannot separate them out. Warmth. Release. Acceptance. Home. A hand reaching out, giving, asking. Perhaps two hands.

She says to Carl, "Do you think Daddy knew?"

"Well, he didn't know about Sam Robbins," Carl says. "Nobody did. But he did know the story about an ancestor fighting at Trafalgar—I remember the old man saying so on the phone. *Gave little Paul a big kick, that,* he said."

"And that's why Daddy called his yacht Victory," Molly says.

"What yacht?" says Russell.

Molly says, "There's a photograph—I haven't shown you yet." She sees in her mind her father standing beside his model boat, laughing at the camera. She wonders whether he looked at all like Sam Robbins.

In a kind of reflex, her hands move to the desk and push the little piece of the *Victory*'s flag back, very gently, into its folded covering.

Mr. Waterford says, "There's one thing I should remind you about—that little object is very valuable. I checked the price that the other piece of the flag went for, at that sale in London, and it was forty-six thousand pounds. That's about eighty thousand dollars. With the inscriptions in your book as provenance, you'd probably get the same for this one, minus commission."

"Wow!" Russell says.

"We couldn't sell it!" Molly says in horror. "It belongs to Sam. It's his bit of Nelson."

She looks up at Carl and sees him nodding his head.

"You're in charge," he says. "Seems to me Sam Robbins gave it to you."

SAM

1832

A<small>FTER OUR</small> A<small>DMIRAL'S FUNERAL AND THE LAST OF OUR SHIP'S</small>
<small>SERVICE IN THAT WAR, WE WERE RELEASED.</small> S<small>O</small> I <small>COULD GO</small>
ashore with what money I had owed to me, and I went first to
my aunt Joan in Chatham. I gave her Uncle Charlie's ring, that
I had worn on the thumb of my left hand for her since Trafalgar.
Poor lady, she missed my uncle sorely for the rest of her days.

Then from Chatham, I went home.

I should say in truth, I went back to what had once been my
home. I had been gone for three years, and I was very different
from the boy who had left. My mother said that when first I
walked in the door, tall and sunburned, wearing a sailor's short

jacket and my hair tied back in a pigtail, she had no idea who I was.

"Until you smiled," she said. "Then you were my Sam."

And her face had lit up like a candlewick catching flame—and the little boy at her knee had taken one look at me and hidden his face in her lap. He was the baby she had had after I left. His name was Charlie.

Nothing in this life stays the same forever. My elder brother Dick had married, and was living with his wife in a cottage nearby. It was not much of a place, but good enough: put up for them by order of the bailiff, who was a good man and had put a new roof on our old house as well. The oldest of my little sisters, Mary, was working up at the great house, in the kitchens. Alice and Beth were still at home, and had grown into pretty girls I hardly recognized.

As for my father, he had had a terrible accident, from a plow horse rearing and kicking him in the head. He had a great scar on his forehead, and though he was still strong and able to work, he was silent and withdrawn—and much easier to live with. Strange, that a cruel accident should turn a fierce man gentle. I was glad of the effect, at any rate, because that made it easier for me to leave my mother again. We all knew that my home was not there with them anymore. My home was a ship at sea.

And so it has been from that day to this, as I put out once more now from Portsmouth, bound for Antigua in the *Vagabond*. As always I leave my heart behind, with my dear wife and daughter, and with my piece of my Admiral's flag, that has been a part of me for so long and ever will be.

Remember that.

Remember that, if you will.

Molly

IN CONNECTICUT

"GRANDAD," SAYS MOLLY INTO THE TELEPHONE, "WHAT WOULD HAVE HAPPENED TO SAM ROBBINS IF HE DIED AT SEA?"

There is a faint crackling pause from Highgate, where Grandad has by now learned the story of Sam's piece of the flag. Then he says, "Well, if you aren't a corpse tossed overboard in the thick of battle, burial at sea is very moving. Back in Sam's time, the body of a dead seaman would have been sewn up in his hammock, probably by his friends, with a heavy chunk of shot at his feet. Then the ship's company would be drawn up on deck and the captain would read the burial service from his prayerbook. And when he got to the line 'We therefore commit his body to the deep,' the plank that the dead man's body was lying on would be tipped up so that he slid down into the sea."

Molly can see this in her imagination as her grandfather describes it. She shivers at the splash and the sinking down, down, down into the sea, but she tries to remind herself that this is not a person Grandad is describing, but a dead body.

"Um," she says.

As if he were reading her mind, Grandad's faraway voice says, "Just remember that's not Sam we're talking about, just his leftover body. Funerals are really ceremonies to say good-bye to someone who isn't there anymore. And to say thank you."

There is another crackling pause, and he says, "Are you all right, sweetheart?"

"Yes, I am," Molly says. "I really am."

She says to her mother, "Did Daddy have a burial at sea?"

"No, love," Kate says, startled. "We had a memorial service for him at St. Peter's Church in Chelsea, where we were all living then. That was how we said good-bye to him. You were there, but I don't think you understood what it was all about."

Molly says, "I think I'd understand now."

It has been a long sail, in a brisk wind. The sailboat is out beyond the tip of Montauk, tossing in the swells from the ocean. Puffy white clouds scurry across the sky.

Carl yells from the tiller, "Right around here, Moll. We're out past the island—this is the Atlantic Ocean now."

"Okay!" Molly calls back. She is crouched amidships, looking out over the gunwale. "Thank you!"

Carl turns the boat up into the wind, so that the mainsail flaps loudly, and Russell loosens the jib. There is an earsplitting rattling of canvas, and then suddenly, astonishingly, the wind drops for a few moments. The sails hang loose, and all you can hear is a faint breath in the rigging, and the smack of the waves against the side of the boat.

Molly takes a small plastic bag out of the inside pocket of her jacket, and her fingers slip inside it. They come out with the tiny piece of grey-white cloth that spent so long inside the cover of Robert Southey's *The Life of Nelson*, Heinemann edition, London, 1897.

She says softly, "I commit Sam's bit of Nelson to the deep."

Holding the scrap of fabric between her fingertips and thumb, she leans over the edge of the boat and lowers her hand into the water. And as the sea takes it, the scrap of cloth dissolves into a little dark cloud, like a ragged trail of dust, slipping away through the grey water, fading, until it is gone.

Molly says to the sea, "That's for Sam Robbins, and for Daddy."

Far off behind the slap of the waves against the boat she hears a faint echo of distant sound, like the roar of an airplane, like the boom of a gun.

Then the wind picks up again and the mainsail flaps loudly, demandingly. Carl calls from the tiller, "Okay?"

"Okay!" Molly calls back. She smiles at him.

"Let's go home," she says.

AUTHOR'S NOTE

This book is a work of fiction, and the life of Samuel Robbins—
like that of Molly Jennings—is entirely my own invention.

But there really was a Samuel Robbins on board HMS *Victory*
at the Battle of Trafalgar: a ship's boy, age thirteen. Every other
member of the crew who appears in this story was a real person
too; you can find them all listed at the *Victory*'s fascinating Web
site, www.hms-victory.com, and amazingly detailed in *The Men
of HMS Victory at Trafalgar* by John D. Clarke.

There are two wonderfully vivid books about the life Sam
and his shipmates must have led, both written by former seamen: *Sea Life in Nelson's Time* by John Masefield and *Life in*

Nelson's Navy by Dudley Pope. Among the many good biographies of Horatio Nelson himself, my favorites are those by Carola Oman, Christopher Hibbert, Tom Pocock and Ernle Bradford—and, of course, Robert Southey.

Vice-Admiral Lord Nelson did not live to be promoted to full admiral, but I have the assurance of a living rear-admiral of Her Majesty's Navy that one may address any kind of admiral as "Admiral" after using his precise rank the first time. Sam Robbins's encounters with Admiral Nelson are not historical; they came out of my imagination, and I loved writing them. Perhaps I wrote this whole book only for the chance of meeting one of my greatest heroes, just as I was lucky enough to meet Shakespeare in a book called *King of Shadows* and Merlin, long ago, in a sequence called *The Dark Is Rising*. Writers are fortunate people.

GLOSSARY

afterguard

Just as the front end of a ship is called the bow and the back end the stern, the front, middle and rear areas are called fore, midships and after. The afterguard is the name for the members of the crew who man the sails at the rear of the ship.

beat to quarters

A drummer beating to quarters was beating out a rhythmic tune that called the crew to their positions for battle.

belay

In sailing, to belay a line is to make it fast, usually round a cleat. In speech, "belay that" means "pay no attention," or just "stop."

bosun

The boatswain—bosun for short—was one of the most important members of the crew, in charge of many things, including the condition and operation of the ship's boats, sails, rigging, anchors and cables.

bosun's pipe

Round his neck the bosun wore a silver whistle, known always in the Royal Navy as a "call," and for each order issued by an officer, he blew a particular sequence of notes and then shouted the order. This was then repeated throughout the ship by his assistants, the bosun's mates, chosen from the most experienced of the seamen.

capstan

An enormous wooden cylinder, turned by seamen pushing bars that were fitted into holes in the cylinder's top; the capstan was generally used to wind up the anchor cable when pulling up ("weighing") the anchor.

carronade

A short-barrelled gun that fired a very heavy shot, doing enormous damage at close quarters.

cutlass
A short, wide-bladed sword used by seamen against boarders.

dry dock
An enclosed area of water in a dockyard, into which a ship can be floated and the water then pumped out, leaving the ship's exterior dry for repairs.

flagship
A flag officer was—and is—an Admiral, Vice-Admiral, Rear-Admiral or Commodore, and his ship flies his flag of command.

fo'c'sle
Short for "forecastle," the raised deck between the foremast and the bow.

galley
The ship's kitchen, on the main or upper deck.

helmsman
The helm, controlled by the helmsman, moves the rudder, which steers the vessel; the helm is a wheel in a large ship, a tiller in a small sailboat.

maintopmen
The topsails are above the first sails; the topmen work them. Maintopmen work the topsails on the mainmast.

midshipman
A naval officer in training, who might be as young as 14 or as old as 40.

pike
A long wooden spear with an iron tip.

rigging
All the ropes, or lines, on a ship are known collectively as the rigging. Standing rigging supports the masts and the yards (the poles to which square sails are attached); running rigging controls the sails.

sheet
A rope attached to a sail, or to the boom along which a sail is stretched, and hauled to change the angle of the sail. In a dinghy, the mainsheet controls the mainsail, the jibsheet the jib—the smaller sail forward of the mast.

splice the mainbrace
This is the order to serve an extra ration of rum—originally a reward for seamen who had the dangerous job of repairing the mainbrace rope high above the deck.

ABOUT THE AUTHOR

Susan Cooper was born in England and was a reporter and feature writer for the *Sunday Times* in London before coming to live in the United States. Of her books for children, the best known are the five books in the fantasy sequence *The Dark Is Rising*, which have among them won a Newbery Medal, a Newbery Honor, two Carnegie Honors, and several other awards. Her book *King of Shadows* was also short-listed for the Carnegie Medal. Her television screenplays for adults have received two Writers Guild Awards and two Emmy nominations. Susan Cooper has two grown children and lives in Connecticut.